BODIES AND BEACHES

BODIES AND BEACHES

ISBN 978-0-9850695-1-3

Don Yarber

<u>This book is dedicated to the memory of:</u>

Emily Stohl, former proofreader for
The Union County Advocate, for her help
proofreading and her encouragement.

Richard S. Prather, author of the Shell Scott mystery
series. He was truly the King of the P.I. novel. I will
be eternally grateful for his advice and
encouragement.

AIRPLANE BOOKS

This is a work of fiction. Any similarities to
actual persons,
living or dead, is purely coincidental or a figment
of the
author's imagination.

Prologue:

Lightning lit up the skies brilliantly. The flash from the Uzi was dim by comparison, insignificant, like a camera flash. The chatter at close range preceded the clap of thunder.

Rain bounced hard off the gleaming polished top of a red Camaro as the passenger door opened. A tall, lanky, bearded man tossed the smoking Uzi into the back seat, sat down, swung his long legs in, and slammed the door.

"Hit it!" he said to the driver.

The purring engine roared to life and the Camaro skidded sideways in the wet ivy until the drive wheels hit paved surface. The car then disappeared, screaming, down the freeway ramp.

The dying man didn't hear the car scream away. Lights from the freeway exit sign twenty yards away played over the mist-covered ivy, causing a myriad of rainbow circles in his eyes.

He struggled in the wet ivy, pulled himself up, hanging onto a Benjamin Fichus tree till he was on his feet.

When he let go and tried to move, he fell headfirst back into the ivy. Blood from holes in his chest glistened eerily. He struggled with every ounce of energy he had left, managed to stagger out onto the freeway. He lifted both arms as if to say STOP. He didn't hear the hissing of tires from an approaching car. Just as he saw the car emerge from the foggy mist his sphincter muscles relaxed and he was dead when the car hit him.

CHAPTER 2.

I got the call in the middle of a very, very comfortable dream. The phone next to my bed, in my dream, was ringing. I was urging the girl not to answer it. The more she kissed me and whispered sweet nothings in my ear, the faster the phone rang. I was struggling subconsciously with the need to continue versus the need to answer the phone. Eventually reality caught up with me; I realized that the phone was actually ringing.

I rose up on one elbow, cursing the person who had the audacity to awaken me from such a pleasant dream. The voice that answered my gruff hello sounded as if it could have been from the girl in the dream, but distant, hollow.

"Is this Kip Yardley?"

"Yep."

"Mr. Yardley, I've got to talk to you. They killed my brother.."

"Whoa, wait a sec, back up..." I sat up on the bed and turned on a light, fumbling in a nightstand drawer for pencil and paper.

"Start at the top. Who's calling?"

"My name is Starla Lang."

"OK, Mrs. Lang, who killed your brother?"

"It's Miss."

"Huh?"

"I said it's Miss Lang, and I don't know who killed my brother. That's why I am calling you. You are Kip Yardley, the detective, aren't you?"

I am, indeed, Kip Yardley, the detective. The way clients had been avoiding my office lately I was beginning to wonder. After six years on the California Highway Patrol, I had resigned and started my agency on a shoestring. Lately, I had begun to wonder if I wasn't going to have to eat the shoe. Things had been slow.

"Yep, I am he," I said.

After assuring her that indeed I was Kip Yardley, I listened to her story. The highway patrol had called her and told her that a body had been found. A distraught driver had called and told them he had hit someone with his car on the freeway. Identification on the body listed her as next of kin. She made a trip to the morgue in Long Beach to identify the body. It was her brother.

She started crying and I waited patiently for her to get over the sobs. She told me that Toby Smith, a friend of mine, had advised her to call me.

I took her number and a few details and made arrangements to meet her near her apartment.

The place was an old favorite club of mine called the Zanzabuku. I had frequented it after a torturous divorce, met a few nice girls, and had grown accustomed to stopping there on the way back to my apartment for a night cap. I wondered why I had stayed away so long, seeing as how I had been striking out left and right lately, and the Zansabuku had always been a lucky spot for me. Then I thought of Maria and answered my own question.

Maria is a very nice young lady, with dark eyes, dark hair that she wears in a pageboy style, an attractive face, remarkably like that of the late Natalie Wood. I had taken her out and she hounded me for a year, showing up at my apartment, leaving notes on my windshield and messages on my recorder. She wouldn't give up. Not that I wanted her to; she was a very hot number in bed. I was, however, reminded of Clint Eastwood in "Play Misty For Me." The difference was I still went back to her occasionally. I just couldn't turn her off completely.

I parked my Chevy in the small lot behind the joint and walked through the back door, out of bright sunlight into the dark interior of the club, pausing to let my eyes adjust to the dimness. The place was empty except for Jim, the bartender, busily stocking the shelves and coolers. I settled my nearly six foot frame gently on a barstool, pushed back my baseball cap on my head and dropped a couple of bills on the bar.

"Kip, what's kept ya?" Jim asked, putting the last of a case of beer in the cooler.

"I've been wondering that myself," I said. "I used to be pretty lucky here. My luck has turned sour lately."

"Wouldn't have been much better here," Jim said. "Not very many girls hang out here anymore since they shut down the plant."

The plant he referred to was the Buick, Olds, Pontiac plant. At one time it employed 3000 persons.

Japan had cut into the US car market for so many years that General Motors was regrouping, cutting back, and hastily trying to engineer smaller, more economical models to compete.

"How about Maria?" I asked. "Does she still come in?"

Jim grinned. "Hell, man, you know Maria won't give up on you till she gets you in front of a priest!"

"Well, let's hope she doesn't come in today. I'm meeting someone on business."

"Tough luck, Kip," Jim said, pointing towards the rest rooms in the back of the bar. "She's in there."

"Oh, heck!" I said, "I'm outta here. I'll be in the can for a while, Jim. Get rid of her for me."

I left the bar and hurried towards the men's room in the back, but not fast enough. I almost ran into Maria as she came out of the ladies' room. I spread my arms wide, smiled from ear to ear and gathered her in my arms.

"Maria, baby, good to see you!"

"Kip, darling!" She was genuinely glad to see me, and I hugged her, spun her around so that I was looking back at Jim, and motioned with one hand, pointing to her, then the door. Jim winked.

"Excuse me, Doll," I told Maria, "I'll be out in a sec."

I slipped into the men's room and locked myself in a stall. I didn't need Maria interfering with my business today, and I wanted to check out my new client undisturbed by prying eyes. I waited a good ten minutes, flushed the john and let myself out. As I walked back in toward the bar, Jim waved a towel at me and motioned for me to come on in and have a seat.

Maria was gone. Sitting alone in a booth near the front of the place was a nice looking redhead, young, probably in her mid twenties.

She had the kind of pretty good looks that belong to few women. A lot of women are good looking, cute, or sexy looking, but damned few are out-and-out pretty. This one was.

Her eyebrows arched high over the greenest eyes I had ever seen. Her cheekbones were high, slightly pink, and her mouth was painted a lovely pink. She was wearing a shiny pink long sleeve blouse that rippled over gently curving breasts, and was tucked into a gray skirt that didn't quite reach the top of her knees. A long stretch of slender thigh showed under her crossed legs. I hoped this would turn out to be Starla Lang.

I stopped and sat down at my former seat. Jim sidled over and told me the girl in the booth had asked for me. My heart skipped a few beats. It was Starla Lang.

"How'd you get rid of Maria so fast?" I muttered.

"Hell, man, that was easy," Jim said, "I told her you had AIDS."

"Oh well," I muttered, and headed for the booth.

CHAPTER 3

M iss Lang?"
　　She smiled at me, trying hard to be pleasant, but behind the lovely face and beautiful smile I could see the pain in her eyes. I felt an immediate need to hold her, soothe her, and comfort her. Her eyes were slightly puffy as though she had been crying, but her mascara was unsmudged.

"I'm Starla Lang." she said. "You must be Kip Yardley."

"I am he," I said. "Very sorry about your brother, Miss Lang."

"Please call me Starla," she smiled.

"What makes you think I can find your brother's killer?" I asked.

"That's a good question, Mr. Yardley," she replied.

"Kip," I said.

"That's a good question, Kip," she repeated. "The Highway Patrol tells me that it is in the jurisdiction of Orange County Sheriff's Office. The Sheriff's office tells me the Garden Grove police will do the investigation. They tell me the Highway Patrol will handle it, since the death occurred on a freeway which is a state highway."

Her upper lip quivered very slightly as she spoke, indicating that tears were not far beneath the surface of those magnificent green eyes.

"I'm so frustrated," she said. "I took Toby Smith's advice and called you."

"I understand," I said in my most comforting manner. "Bureaucratic nonsense. the old run-around. I'm sure that someone is investigating, however; probably all three."

"Toby told me that you could do a better job, faster," she said. "I want to find my brother's killers as soon as possible."

"Tell me about your brother, Miss Lang, Starla," I said, and pulled a dog-eared notebook and stub of pencil from my Levis pocket.

She told me that her brother was twenty-two years old; he had worked at the GM plant until the big lay-off, and then found a job with the highway department, landscaping the freeways. She went on to tell me about his personality, his girl friends, his ambitions, and that he was her only brother.

Her father had been in the Navy, and though Steve and she had been born in Jacksonville, Florida, they grew up in California, first at San Diego, then Long Beach.

Starla had been five when Steve was born. Her parents had prepared her well for the arrival of a baby brother and she had loved him immediately. There was no jealousy or sibling rivalry. She took care of her brother as if he were a baby doll, always watching out for him, picking up after him, and doing favors for him.

Starla never minded the time her father had devoted to Steve; she was very close with her mother, and they spent as much time together as did Steve and her father.

She went on to say that Steve had changed in the past month preceding his death. He had become very secretive, withdrawn from his normal jolly personality. He had mentioned to his girlfriend, Donna, that he was going to have enough money to marry her soon. He wanted to invest in a car dealership.

"Do you have a recent picture of Steve?" I asked.

"Just this one of him and Donna at the beach," she said as she handed me a gold-framed picture. From behind the glass a young couple looked out at me. He was blond, appeared to be over six feet tall, good looking and built like a weight lifter. Donna, the girl in the picture, was cute, very tan and well endowed, long legs, large boobs, and a small waist.

At my request Starla gave me Donna's address and phone number, and Steve's address. She told me that the Garden Grove police had asked for Donna's address and phone number also. I had a hunch that they were more interested in the case than it might appear.

CHAPTER 4

We sipped Corona beers from iced mugs as we talked. An hour passed very quickly and when I said good-bye and offered to take her home it was after noon. She declined the ride, saying that she had her car in front and had some shopping to do.

I paid Jim for the beers and left the quiet, cool club for the afternoon heat and traffic.

I worked my way to the 605 Freeway southbound, my Chevy air conditioner barely working. The sun shining through the passenger window had the temperature inside the car at

boiling. The sheepskin seat covers were hot against my bare arms and I was glad I had worn Levis and a tee shirt.

Unlike detectives in the movies and on television, I hardly ever wear a suit, rarely carry a gun (although I have a permit) and can't afford a better car than my Chevy, let alone a Ferrari or Corvette.

My income over the past three years after leaving the CHP has just barely averaged twenty grand. That paid my rent, kept my name in the yellow pages and bought my beer and food. I spend very little on clothes and cars.

The address that I got for Donna turned out to be a neatly decorated old apartment building in the less expensive area of Seal Beach, not far from SAM'S seafood cafe. I decided to stop and get a bite to eat at SAM'S.

A large sign out in front looks like a swordfish made of blue neon with the words "SAM'S SEAFOOD" in red neon. SAM's has been in the same spot, serving the same good food and drinks for at least thirty years. Even though it sets right on the waterfront, the booths are on the street side and kitchen on the waterside. I had often wondered why they didn't remodel and make the booths look out over the water, but the place remained exactly the same through the years.

It was early afternoon, not yet three. I didn't know if I would be able to get a meal or not but the beer was wearing off and I was hot and thirsty. I needed something cool to drink.

I made my way through dangling fishnets filled with corks, baubles, shells, and the usual nautical trinkets, and into a cool bar. The long wooden bar was made of a progression of hatch covers coated with an inch thick resin. Embedded in the resin were coins from all over the world.

I ordered a Mai Tai and turned to watch the Dodgers and Mets game on the television above the end of the bar.

Vin Scully was saying, "And from Vero Beach, Florida, where the Dodgers drop their third consecutive spring training game to the Mets by the score of 13 to 3, this is Vin Scully for Don Drysdale and the Dodger Baseball Network, reminding you to tune in tomorrow for the Dodgers and the Mets in game three of this spring training series. Until then, Good Day!"

So the game was over. I sipped my Mai Tai and absently watched a few minutes of commercials and then the three o'clock news.

The news was of the shooting of a Southern California man, Hoss Macmillan, kingpin of at least a dozen topless or nude bars, and allegedly involved in drugs, prostitution, and a number of other things in the Los Angeles area.

Hoss had been on his way back to his 40 acre hidden ranch that he affectionately called TARA. He had been riding in the back of his limo. The driver had gotten out to close the gate and three men had opened fire with shotguns and nine millimeter assault rifles, shooting through the closed back window of the limo. The deputy coroner reported that Hoss's body had been hit twenty times by 9mm slugs and shot from a 12 gauge shotgun.

The driver could not identify any of the men and police had no clues at this time to their identities or motive. Speculation was that Hoss had reneged on a dope deal.

The interesting part was that Hoss had been a motorcycle officer for the California Highway Patrol for seven years before getting into the topless and nude bar business. CHP stated that he was dismissed in 1983. No reason was given for his dismissal, but he had since served two years for assault on a CHP officer, unlawful flight to avoid prosecution and resisting arrest. The IRS, for possible prosecution on income tax evasion charges, had recently audited his books.

Hoss was a legend around the LA area. At six feet seven inches and 290 pounds, he had wrestled professionally, was a black belt in Karate, and was infamous for bar fights before joining the CHP. He had served in Viet Nam and had received the Bronze Star.

Recently he had been granted an uncontested divorce from his wife after allegedly threatening to cut off her breasts and make her eat them.

I listened intently to the part about the CHP, but was only half listening to the rest. I had known Hoss since college and I knew his reputation without being reminded by the television.

It saddened me to think that the guy had been killed. I don't hold any special love for drugs, prostitutes, or wife mutilators, and I don't frequent topless bars. Viet Nam heroes, however, occupy a special place in my heart; I have a brother who served there.

I finished my Mai Tai and left the coolness of the bar for the dining room. A cute waitress showed me the way to a table and I ordered red snapper, coleslaw, and fries. The order came sooner than I expected and I wolfed down the food, chased it with iced tea, paid my bill and left. From a pay phone outside I dialed Donna's number.

I let the phone ring a dozen times, then decided to drive by and ring the doorbell just in case she had been in the shower when I called.

CHAPTER 5

Knocking on the door at 2727 13th Avenue, I watched an old woman sweeping the sidewalk next door. She stopped and peered at me like I was a burglar trying to pick the lock, then resumed her sweeping. No one answered my insistent knocking and I was just turning to leave when the old lady spoke.

"She ain't home!"

No kidding, I muttered to myself.

"Do you know when she will be back?" I asked.

"She works on the paper in the afternoon and goes to school nights."

"What paper is that?" I asked.

"The Surf Sound, of course!" She answered.

"Of course," I said.

To myself I muttered something about snooty old bags sweeping side walks, but thanked her anyway.

"Do you know what time she usually gets home?" I asked.

"Well, that boy usually brings her home about eleven at night."

I pulled out the picture Starla had given me.

"This boy?"

"Yep, that's the one," she grinned, "good looker, that one."

"Yes ma'am," I said. Good and dead, I said to myself.

At a telephone booth on 13th and Pacific Coast Highway I found the address for the Surf Sound paper. It was a weekly tabloid that was subsidized entirely by local advertisers, distributed from free news racks in local stores. The address was 1501 Main, only a few blocks away, so I turned the Chevy around and headed towards Main.

I parked in front of a brick faced building with large glass windows. A sign painted in black letters told me this was the Surf Sound.

Inside the building was an office front with three desks, divided by gray office dividers. A reporter's desk was in the front. A sign on the reporter's desk told me I had the right office. Engraved on a bronze plaque was "DONNA MAE WILSON".

Donna Mae, I thought should be Daisy May by the picture of her in the bikini.

I looked around for anyone to talk to, but all three desks were unoccupied. No one was in the office. I walked through a twelve-foot hallway with "Men's" on one side and "Lady's" on the other and pondered about a newspaper that misspelled Ladies'.

I opened a door at the end of the hall and immediately was engulfed with the clacking sound of a typesetter in action. The man at the console was in his fifties, slightly bald and wore thick glasses.

"Excuse me, sir?" I said.

He didn't look up. I surmised that his hearing was probably as bad as his eyesight so I walked to where I was sure he could see me and stuck out my hand, moved it up and down. He glanced at me but didn't acknowledge my presence. Instead he kept typing away at the console, with each stroke the ancient typesetter clacked out another character on the lead strip.

When the strip reached its maximum length it clanged into a steel tray hanging by a piece of wire next to the console. I wondered what the environmental protection boys would think about this lead spitting dinosaur showering the area with lead dust and contaminating everything within fifty feet, including the operator.

Finally he turned and looked at me, flipped a switch on the console to turn off the clacking monster, scratched his bald head and grinned a false teeth grin.

"What can I do for you today, sir?"

"I'm looking for Donna Mae Wilson."

"Oh, she went across the street to get some lunch," he said, then arched his eyebrows and asked, "Who are you?"

"I just need to ask her some questions," I replied. I have learned over the years not to identify myself unless absolutely necessary. People have different feelings about private investigators asking questions.

If they think they personally can benefit by answering, or if they think you are there to benefit a friend of theirs, they will open up. If they don't think either of the above, they clam up.

"Catch her on her lunch hour then," he said, "I don't pay her to answer stranger's questions; she gets paid to ask them, not answer them."

He turned the clacking monster back on, adjusted the copy on a holder and started to type again. Interview completed.

I backed out of the typesetting room, made my way back to the front and out the door. Across the street was a tiny cafe squeezed between a hardware store and a clothing store. Blue curtains hung in small wood-framed windows, blue, flowered wallpaper hung on the walls. Four booths lined the left wall, an aisle ran down the middle and a counter with stools was on my right. In the booth next to the window sat Donna Mae Wilson. I would have known her in a dark closet.

The tee-shirt she wore had a picture of a surfer riding a wave. On his shoulder was a newspaper bag like the paper boys use. On the bag was "SURF SOUND" in old English script. The part of the shirt that depicted the bag was across her left breast and it looked strangely as if it might have been a real bag, full of newspapers.

"Donna Mae Wilson?" I asked.

"That's me!" she said, more like she didn't know it was she until I told her.

"Hi, my name is Kip Yardley," I said, "I'm a friend of Starla's."

"Oh," she said, "Starla said you were good looking but I think she was understating the truth!"

"Thanks," I said, blushing.

I've never thought of myself as being good looking. Come to think of it, I've never thought of myself at all when it comes to looks. I am six feet and one seventy pounds, small waist and medium build. My eyebrows are thin, some of them grow straight out after they escape the scar tissue over my steel blue eyes, the result of boxing and bar room brawls. I had boxed in Boys Club and carried it over into the Navy. During the Navy and for a few years after I had been the first to swing if there was any indication that someone wanted to fight.

I had mellowed out a lot in the past ten years.

"Well, what can I do for you?" she asked.

"I would like to ask you a few questions about Steve," I said.

Her demeanor turned immediately misty. Too immediate, I thought. It was like she could turn on the crocodile tears when it pleased her. I had a first impression that she wasn't going to spend the rest of her life grieving for Steve Lang.

"I'll try," she sniffled, "I really am hurt by Steve's death. We talked about getting married."

"Just what did Steve say about getting married?" I asked, "Did he mention where he expected to get the money Starla told me about?"

"He didn't talk about that much," she said, "Only that he was onto something big and that as soon as he could find some guy he was looking for that he would have a lot of money coming. He planned to buy into a car dealership; that was his dream."

"What guy?" I asked, my attention suddenly spiked.

"Well, he didn't mention a name, just that he was going to try to make a connection with this guy and that it would bring him a lot of money. He mentioned $200 thousand as the amount."

I thought about that briefly.

There are damned few places or legal deals that will get a guy two hundred grand in cash. Loans, of course, are legal. The only collateral Steve Lang had was his car, worth a total of maybe five grand. Not much chance he was being financed. That left drug deals, bank robberies, and damned few other things. My mind was hitting a snag, bells started to tinkle, but I couldn't grasp it.

"Who were Steve's enemies?" I asked, "Who would have anything to gain by killing him?"

"Come on," she said, "Steve didn't have any enemies. As a matter of fact, everybody I know liked him. He had a lotta girl friends before we met."

"Then who were his friends?" I queried.

"Well, we hung out at the beach a lot. Steve surfed and played volleyball with a bunch of guys."

"Any names? Anyone special that he talked to a lot?"

"There was one guy," she mused, "I remember him talking to this guy. It was about two weeks ago. I think they called him Hare."

"Hare? As in rabbit?" I asked, "Or Hare, short for Harry?"

"No, his name wasn't Harry, I don't think. I think it was just a nickname."

"Do you know where he lives?"

"No, but you could ask about him at the pool."

I knew she was talking about the Belmont Shores pool. Used in the 1984 Olympic games, the pool is a hundred yards from the ocean in an older section of Long Beach, commonly referred to as "the shores."

Every beach bum who lived in Southern California was aware of the shores. The surf was not worth mentioning since it was a south facing beach, but the girls that sat watching the boys play volleyball were well worth mentioning.

"Did Steve ever mention drugs as a possible means of getting money?" I asked.

"No way, Jose!" she said. "Steve never used drugs, and neither do I."

"O.K.," I hastened, "just wondered." "I bet," I said to myself.

I thanked her for the information, promised to let her know if I found out anything worth mentioning and stood up to leave.

"How much is Starla paying you?" she asked.

"Not enough!" I said.

"Well, come and see me again," she smiled. "Maybe I can help pay some of your expenses, somehow." She emphasized the word somehow.

I bet you would, I thought, and walked out.

CHAPTER 6

Seal Beach is about a twenty minute drive south of the shores. I knew it was getting late, and there probably wouldn't be anyone at the beach at this time of day, but I drove north up Pacific Coast Highway and turned left on 2nd street, over the bridge and left again on 14th. A right turn on Ocean Boulevard brought me to the beach. At the parking lot, I pulled the Chevy into a stall, got out and stuck a quarter in the meter. That would keep the meter maids off my back for fifteen minutes.

As I suspected, the beach was nearly deserted. A few die hard sunbathers lay next to the wall behind the pool building. One group of four, two girls and two burly looking guys were playing volleyball. I walked towards them.

The sun was still hot and so was the sand. I felt it sliding into my shoes, so I stopped and took them off. Fifteen feet from the volleyball court, I sat down in the sand. I watched the game. Muscles rippled across the bare chests of the guys, titties bounced on the girls. After the game, one girl walked straight towards me, then stopped and plopped down on a blanket.

"Do any of you know a guy named Hare?" I asked.

I got a cold stare from the girl on the blanket, then the biggest of the two guys walked toward me.

"What do you want with him?" He asked, curling up his lip and staring down at me. If there's one thing that gets my goat it's a goat that curls its lip.

"I just need to ask him a few questions," I replied.

"Maybe he don't want to hear them," the girl said.

"Maybe he could tell me that," I said.

"Maybe you don't hear too good, pal," the big guy said. "Besides, you shouldn't talk to a lady like that."

I crossed my legs under me and rose from the sand in one motion.

"Show me a lady, and I'll be careful what I say."

I knew the punch was coming a full two seconds before he actually threw it. First I saw the look in his eyes, then I saw the muscles bunch up in his right arm. The punch might just as well have been mailed by U. S. Postal service.

I shifted left and blocked right with an outside block that let the punch slide by harmlessly. He was too close for a kick, so I pivoted behind him, gave him a hard elbow in the kidneys. At the same time, I was hooking my right foot behind his, and with a slight pulling motion of my foot, sent him sprawling in the sand. He bounced up with surprising speed, but not quick enough. I had time to kick him in the groin. As he doubled over, I shifted back and with my right foot placed a roundhouse kick on the left side of his head. This time he didn't get up.

I had been watching the other guy out of the corner of my eye. As he lunged at me I sprang backwards. He missed grabbing me, but as he went by, I stooped and with both hands shoveled sand in his face.

He spun away from me, yelling and rubbing his eyes with his hands. I put my foot in the small of his back and pushed him hard. He tripped over the first guy and fell heavily to the sand.

I pulled a card from my wallet, walked to the girl on the blanket who was staring open-mouthed. I bent and pulled the top of her bikini away from her tan belly, dropped my card in, and backed away.

"If anyone remembers to ask Hare to call me," I said, "that's my number."

I turned and walked back, picked up my shoes and listening intently for the rush of footsteps, headed back to my car. I got all the way to the sidewalk by the parking lot and no one had come after me. Maybe they had had enough. I glanced back once. The two girls were bent over the goons, consoling them. The one I had given the card to pulled it from her bikini and handed it to the big guy.

I got in the Chevy and left. Three minutes still showed on the parking meter.

CHAPTER 7.

That night I dreamed of the beach. In my dreams, the two guys who had chosen to fight were holding me down while the girl pulled hands full of sand and black pubic hairs from her bikini bottom and stuffed them in my mouth. I was choking and gasping for air. A huge fist was clamped over my mouth and strong fingers pinched my nostrils. I struggled desperately, fighting for breath.

When I woke up I was sweating profusely. I got up, took a shower, straightened the messed covers and got back in bed. The clock on my nightstand ticked two o'clock.

I woke up again at five. I was awake immediately, an idea ringing like a bell in my head. The ways to make a fast 200 grand were:

1. Drugs
2. Rob a bank
3. Kill someone.

Had Steve Lang masterminded the Hoss MacMillan hit?

I got up, showered again hastily, shaved and pulled on some of my better clothes: a pair of cream colored slacks, a blue blazer with a light blue turtleneck under it. I made myself breakfast of scrambled eggs, English muffin and coffee, ate it ravenously, locked the door and left.

My first stop was at the Garden Grove offices of the California Highway Patrol.

Toby Smith was a friend that I had known since college. He was president of my fraternity, Chi Gamma Iota. The vets. I had not intended to join a fraternity, but the vets were just a bunch of guys that had served at least two years in the military. They were not spoiled brats who attended college at the expense of moms and dads, rather were getting a measly $110 a month from the GI bill like I was.

The vets believed that any boot camp for any branch of the service was hazing enough, so there was none of that nonsense. The great part of the Vets fraternity was age. Most of the guys were at least twenty-one, which meant they could buy booze legally. That meant that most of the sororities wanted exchanges with Chi Gamma Iota.

Toby was a likable redhead with protruding front teeth and freckles. Howdy Doody was a close cousin. But for some reason the guy was a hit with the ladies. He had a high-pitched voice, not feminine, but raspy, and a laugh that could best be described as a whinny.

His personality was first class, however, and I liked him immediately. He helped me get acquainted with a lot of girls. He broke me of being too bashful to ask for a date, and after a football game one night announced to the entire bleacher section over the P.A. System that there was a party at my place.

The two-room bachelor apartment couldn't hold all the people that showed up, and soon the pool was full of clothed coeds, everyone with a beer in their hand, and everyone having a helluva time.

"Hi, buddy," he greeted me as I walked in.

"Hi, Toby," I smiled. "Question, ol' buddy."

"I can't answer it if you don't ask it," he laughed.

"What do you know about a guy named MacMillan who used to ride the motorcycle patrol?"

"Oh, Hoss?" He grinned. "I know he's dead. That's about all."

He wanted to know what I had that tied to Hoss's death.

"I'm not sure, Toby," I answered, truthfully. "Can you give me what you have without getting in trouble?"

Toby poured us coffee from a Mister Coffee Maker and sat down at a computer terminal.

"Just a second," he said. He punched a few keys on the keyboard and stared as the screen rolled and rolled.

"I'll make you a deal," he said. "I'll let you see this if you promise to let me in on anything you find. Deal?"

"Deal!" I said.

He moved his chair and scooted up another for me. We read the screen together. It was not a lot more than I already knew. When we finished, Toby said he had something that wasn't on the computer.

"His ex-wife recently remarried."

"To whom?" I asked.

"I don't know the name, but it's probably on record at city hall. Some biker type."

As I prepared to leave Toby startled me.

"He probably had it coming, but whoever did it is a dead man."

"What makes you say that?" I asked.

"Hoss had friends all over. In jail, out of jail," he waved his hand at an imaginary world. "A hundred bikers would gladly off Hoss's killer just for the hell of it!"

Nice people. I thanked him and left. Next stop, TARA.

Hoss had paid $5.5 million for the 35 acre ranch he called TARA, and at California's standards, he got a bargain. Nestled in a valley off Soledad Canyon, Tara had two swimming pools, one for people, one for horses. A nine- hole golf course surrounded the back acres. Tennis courts stretched lazily behind the twenty room mansion. The place was completely walled in by a 12 foot slump stone wall. Two feet of tangled barbed wire with razor blade strands donned the top of the wall.

To get in you had to pass through the main gate, a sixteen-foot wide passageway, with two 8-foot iron gates that opened in, controlled by hydraulic cylinders. One gate opened at a time, depending on whether you were coming or going, and if you were exiting, you ran over spikes set in concrete, placed strategically so that cars trying to get through the OUT gate would have ruined tires.

The house itself was built like a Mediterranean Castle, not unlike the castle W. R. Hearst had built at San Simeon, but not as big.

I pulled up to the guard shack and honked. No one answered. Yellow police tape hung loosely from the gates. I backed out, parked the Chevy further up Soledad Canyon Road under the overhanging branches of an eucalyptus tree. The branches of the tree hung nearly to the pavement edge and by rearranging a few I was quickly able to hide my car from all but a careful observer.

I walked back to the gate and pounded on a wooden door of the guard structure, thinking that someone might ignore a car honking but respond to a knock. Still no one answered. I got out some picks and went to work on the lock. Someone had lubricated the lock recently, and with a little pressure on the turning pick, the tumblers moved and the door swung open on silent hinges.

I went in, shading my eyes to adjust to the dim interior, stood perfectly still for a few minutes, then inspected the door to see if I had set off any silent alarms. At the top of the door, two small plastic boxes with metal strips and wires running down the sides told me that the door had an alarm. My heart raced until I noticed the wires had been clipped about waist high. I breathed easier.

The alarm had been incapacitated prior to my arrival. I glanced around to see if there was a way into the grounds from this room. At the back of the cubicle was a window opening on the driveway side, apparently a foul weather check point. I felt along the edge of it in the dimness, searching for another alarm wire.

Convinced there was none, I opened the window a crack and looked out. No one was in sight. I started to open it further when I heard the sound of tires barely squeaking as a car turned off the main road to the blacktop. I let the window drop and waited. The sound stopped and for a split second I thought the car was gone. Just as I raised the window again, I caught a glimpse of a black Cadillac disappearing up the blacktop, past where I had left my car. I opened the window and eased myself out one leg at a time.

I knew the house was around the second curve of the drive and the drive was lined with cypress trees growing close together. I was relatively sure no one could see me from the house.

After walking to a point on the second curve where I thought I might be seen from the house, I stopped and surveyed the situation. To my right was an open field, a few cactus plants, then a creek that appeared to wind toward the house, evident by a line of shrubbery greener than the cactus and wild oats in the field.

The day was not extremely hot, but I was sweating in the turtleneck and jacket. I took the jacket off and tied the sleeves together around my waist.

I thought that if I could get in the creek, I would be able to follow it up to a point where I could scramble to the house without being seen. I stepped over a low, crumbling rock wall and sprinted towards the creek.

ZZZZZINNNGG. Something whistled past my ear, and I heard the "crack" of a rifle behind me and to my left. I lunged to my right and dove, hands in front of me. I landed in a cactus patch and grimaced as spines pricked my hands and chest. I heard another crack from behind me. The noise wasn't any louder and I did not hear a whistle this time so I knew the sniper wasn't chasing me. I managed to scramble to my feet, ripping my slacks on cactus needles. I sprinted five huge steps then dove again.

This time I felt a shock in my right arm as my shoulder hit a huge rock that had been hidden behind wild oats. I rolled again, and crawled behind the rock, pain sizzling like hot bacon in my shoulder.

I squeezed as close to the ground as I could and crawled around the edge of the rock. I thought I saw movement a hundred yards away, beyond the road and in the row of cypress trees. I lay there, my pulse pounding in my temples, mouth dry, waiting. When I dared look again I saw sunlight glint off something further up the row of trees. My assailant was moving towards the house. Soon he would be in the bend of road where my rock cover would be useless.

I momentarily thought about my 9mm Star that was in a shoulder holster in the trunk of my car. Good place for it, I thought. But a pistol at this range is useless anyway. I peered around the rock again and watched the Cypress trees ahead of where I had seen the glint of sunlight. Bushes moving slightly told me he was moving.

If he was moving he couldn't be sighting, so now was my time to move.

I sprang to my feet and ran towards the creek bed. As I stumbled into the dry creek bed I realized that even though I was unarmed, against a man with a high-powered rifle, the edge had shifted ever so slightly my way. I knew where he was; he could only guess where I was.

I sprinted up the creek bed, running low to avoid the brush. As I suspected, the creek followed the curvature of the road. The last curve in the road actually crossed the creek. There was a small wooden bridge, just wide enough for one car at a time to pass over.

I stumbled on a rock and heard the stones clatter just as I ducked under the bridge. I stood there, hunched over, breathing heavily, gasping for breath and listening. I heard nothing.

Suddenly I saw a man appear not six feet from me. He had jumped off the bridge, right in my face. An AK47 burped flames and I heard the slugs chewing at the bridge floor inches over my head. I hit him at the knees with my right shoulder and felt the pain shoot all the way down to my wrist. He went flying backwards, a spray of slugs went skyward, the chatter of the AK47 was loud in my ears.

I scrambled as fast as I could up over his outstretched body, trying to grab the gun. As my eyes passed his belt I saw an automatic pistol, a Star 9mm.

Just like mine, I thought. I grabbed at it and it sprang to my fist from the clamshell holster. Just like mine. I put the barrel under his chin and yelled at the top of my lungs.

"FREEZE!"

He started to laugh.

"What the hell's funny?" I asked, "I've got the drop on you and you're laughing? Are you nuts?"

"I'm laughing, senor," he said calmly, "because the gun you have at my throat is not loaded."

I raised my eyes slowly till I could see the butt of the gun. There wasn't a clip in it. Then I noticed a small scratch on the butt, where I had opened a beer bottle with it once.

It was my gun!

Before I could react, my opponent jumped back like a cat and pointed the barrel of the AK47 at my midsection.

"Now, don't try anything funny, senor," he said. "I missed you once, but I won't miss at this range."

"Why aren't you shooting then?" I asked.

"Don't tempt me," he said. I didn't.

He motioned with the gun barrel and I walked in the direction he was pointing.

As we walked he told me that it had occurred to him that I might be worth more to his boss alive than dead.

"You a cop?" he asked, grinning through tobacco stained teeth. His swarthy, acne scarred complexion glistened brightly in the morning sun.

When I didn't answer, he swore at me and said he could take me in a fair fight anytime. Sure, I thought, as long as you have the gun.

"And if I disagree?" I asked.

"It's your life, amigo," he laughed.

We headed straight for a large barn situated 50 yards from the house. I decided that discretion was the better part of valor, and kept walking ten yards ahead of my captor with my hands on my head.

"How did you get my gun?" I asked.

"Very easy," he said, "I just popped open the trunk of your car with a tire iron and helped myself."

I'd like to pop open your head with a tire iron, I thought. He must have been in the big Cadillac that I had seen pass slowly. I should have paid more attention. Oh, well. No need crying over spilled milk. Spilled blood? Maybe.

We reached the barn and he ordered me to open a huge sliding door and go inside. The place smelled. Not like a barn should smell, not the odor of horse manure and animal sweat, but a different smell. More like burning alfalfa. I suddenly realized what it was. Marijuana!.

My captor closed the door behind us without taking his beady eyes off me. The interior of the barn was suddenly dim. I didn't feel like taking a burst of 9mm in my backside so I stopped and waited for instructions.

"Over there," he said, motioning with the gun. I moved in the direction indicated and we walked through a tack room and another door into a stable that had been converted into a make-shift office. A battered old steel desk sat in the middle, a bare bulb hung over the desk. Behind it sat the ugliest human being I had ever seen in my life.

"Look what I found, Hair!" my captor said.

So this was Hare. Or Hair, correctly. He was at least six two, judging from the way his body sat in the chair and above the desk. He was covered with hair. The only part of his face that wasn't hairy was his nose and a slit where his eyes were. Hair even hung down over the small lips. He reminded me of a cartoon character, Yosemite Sam.

He looked up at me and scowled.

"Who the hell are you?" he asked. "And what the hell are you doing here?"

"Might I ask the same thing of you?" I replied.

"No, dammit," he said. "I'll ask the questions. If you know what's good for you, you'll answer 'em."

"Ask away!" I said, hurriedly.

"Who are you?"

"Kip Yardley," I answered.

"What brings you to TARA?" he asked, cleaning his ugly fingernails on hair covered fingers with a knife commonly called a frog-sticker.

"I wanted to see Scarlet," I said, and immediately was sorry for being cute. Mexicali Rose, behind me, clipped me hard in the kidneys with the butt of the AK47. I went down on my knees, seeing stars, then pulled myself up slowly, holding to the edge of the desk.

"Wise guys finish last, mister," Hair said. He pointed the blade of the knife at my midsection and grinned.

"We can remove that aching kidney for you if you'd like."

"No thanks," I grunted, catching my breath.

"I repeat, what brings you to TARA?"

I thought as fast as my pain-riddled brain would allow and decided that there was no future to lying and nothing but pain to gain from being a smart-ass.

"I wanted to talk to someone about Hoss's death. I'm working a case."

"You a cop?"

"Private," I said.

"A private dick?" He laughed. "Well that's good cause I never liked the idea of burning a real cop."

"Look, just tell Manual Labor here that I don't appreciate being shot at or whacked in the kidneys, and that if I ever see his ugly ass outside of captivity, I intend to injure his head, not his kidneys."

I glanced behind me in time to see the rifle butt descending towards my skull. I pivoted, spun and launched a hard back kick that caught the attacker in the mid-section. His breath whooshed out of him.

The next instant I was suspended in the air, my shirt front bunched in a huge hairy fist. I would never have believed that a man so big could move so fast. Hair had rounded the desk, grabbed me and lifted with one big hand, shoving me hard against the plank boards of the barn.

"Well, smart ass, you may have stumbled onto something you had no business knowing," he said. As he lowered me to the floor he snickered and said, "If so, it'll cost you dearly. Like forever, man."

"Cover him, Ernesto!" he said to the other man. "Don't let him near enough to kick you again, got it? If you have to, blow the sonofabitch away!"

He returned to the chair, scratched a huge hairy chest with one hand and sat down.

"Now where were we?" he asked. "Oh, yeah. What kind of case would bring a private eye way out here? The cops swarmed all over this place for three days."

"A kid I know got himself shot," I said. "He bragged about doing a job that was going to pay big before he was hit."

"Aahh, and you thought the job may have been the Hoss hit?" he said, grinning and showing a row of uneven rotting teeth. The guy wasn't as dumb as he was ugly.

"You got it," I said.

"Well," he grinned, "what have you found out?"

"I haven't found out anything that I didn't already know," I said. "So why don't you just let me pull out of here, I'll forget Jose shot at me. I won't even mention that there's a hairy ape holed up in Hoss's barn smoking dope."

Again I underestimated Hair's speed. He was out of the chair, leaned across the desk and had a strangle hold on my windpipe before I could react. Either I was getting slow or this guy had trained with Bruce Lee.

"Let me tell you something, asshole!" he grimaced. "I have never liked you pretty boy types. Not because of me being ugly, but because you always got all the pretty girls and guys like me got what was left. One more word about my looks and I'll carve that pretty face of yours up and feed the pieces to the ducks!"

He shoved me backwards and as I fell I got the butt of the rifle between my shoulders. Pain puked its way through my chest and the taste of bile was strong in my mouth as I hit the dirt floor.

"Tie him up, Ernesto, and put him in the hole."

"Let's bury him permanent like," Ernesto said.

"No, just do as I say," Hair snarled. "The boss will decide what to do with him."

I was still hurting as Ernesto handed the rifle to Hair and jerked my arms up behind my back. My hands were tied together and my feet pulled up. Three quick loops around my ankles and back around my wrists and I was hog-tied all in a matter of thirty seconds.

Hair walked around me and with a sweeping motion of his foot brushed hay aside. He picked up an iron ring and effortlessly lifted a hatch made of two by fours, exposing a dark hole beneath it.

Ernesto stooped and grabbed my ankles, pulling me towards the hole. He pushed with his foot in the small of my back.

I felt myself falling for what seemed like eternity. With a crunch of rib bones and shoulder, I hit a dirt floor. I lay still, trying to catch my breath.

The hatch closed above me and I found myself in total darkness, my mind reeling, spinning. Pain, like a fog bank on a cotton field, smothered over me.

Chapter 8

I woke up. My mind was busily trying to figure out what had happened and where the hell I was. I lay still, trying not to put an undue strain on my aching shoulder. It was cool in the hole and I let myself relax as much as possible. I realized that I was alone in the barn. There was no sound of any kind coming from the floor above me. My eyes became accustomed to the darkness and I could make out a very dim outline of things around me. I tried to sit up but the way I was tied made it impossible.

The lack of circulation in my wrists had long since turned my fingers into pins and needles that ached with every movement. I forced myself to relax again.

There is a technique in Martial Arts called "to the wall." Simply stated, it is the meditating technique that allows one to completely disregard outside influences, blank out pain, and meditate. I had practiced the technique many times prior to sparring with my Sensei. I always pictured a beautiful water fountain with the water shooting up six to eight feet and falling crystal clear back to a point where it disappeared.

Slowly I reached the point of total concentration, total meditation.

I don't know how much longer I lay there. Eventually I found that I could roll onto my back, arms behind me, legs drawn up behind, then onto my stomach and chest again.

It appeared as though the room was fifteen feet or so across and maybe twice that in length, a large underground storage place. At the far end of the room I could see what appeared to be a light of some sort, at least a glow.

Thinking that it might be coming from outside sunlight, I rolled towards it. On the third roll I bumped against something with a thump. I rolled over once more to see what I had hit.

I could barely make out the object. It was a box, maybe two feet long, a foot deep and eight inches wide. I rolled till I could grab the box with my hands behind me and lifted it. It moved freely which told me it was empty; probably an old army ammo box. I ran my tingling fingers over it. A jab of pain sent a message to my aching brain that I had found a sharp object.

I probed until I found the object; it was a nail! Shifting to my elbows, and twisting my legs and body, I managed to get my hands in a position to snag the nail on the ropes.

I started chewing away at the ropes, snagging the nail, then pulling, snagging and pulling. I had no idea what progress I was making, but I knew that if I had enough time I could eventually work my way through the ropes.

I worked at it hard, sweating in the cool, damp hole for a long time. Seconds turned into minutes and minutes into hours and still relentlessly I snagged the nail and pulled. When I tired completely out, I rested, lying on my side, and counted to one thousand slowly.

I couldn't keep on. My fingers were numb, I had missed the rope and jabbed the nail into my wrists three times. I wondered absently how long it had been since I had a tetanus booster. I couldn't think, my brain had reached a point of overload, handling the pain and the effort of meditation. I relaxed as much as I could.

I must have drifted off to sleep; when I woke I felt rested but stiff as a board and sore as a boil. My muscles ached from the restraint, my wrists hurt and my shoulder hurt. A dull ache spread outward from between my shoulders into my arms, and up my neck into my head. My mouth was dry and I needed desperately to urinate.

My kidneys were on standby, bladder at the bursting point. I knew that I had to get out of here soon. One of two things would happen, either I would starve to death or the goons that put me here would come back and finish the job. I was beginning to think that either of those two would be an improvement.

I started again on the ropes, snagging and tugging. On the third try I strained at the ropes and felt something give. The ropes felt loser on my wrists. I flexed my fingers as far as possible and tugged at the ropes. No luck. I worked my fingers around until I found a loose end and backed away from it by touch till I reached a knot.

I tried prying on the knot and found to my utter relief that one end of the rope was going to pull through. I pulled on it, every tug a torment. Eventually the loose end slipped through the loop and I started on the next loop. In desperation I yanked my hands apart and the rope slipped, leaving my hands a foot or so apart.

I could now use my hands, even though they were still tied together, to test the ropes on my ankles. After a few minutes I had my ankles untied and could stretch my legs. After several hours of being curled, my hamstrings felt as if they would snap. Fire blazed its way up my legs as I stretched them.

I managed to get my feet under me and stood up. I staggered a few steps till I got my balance and stood still. I stumbled towards the glow that I had seen earlier. I tripped over something and fell headlong, hands still behind me, to the floor.

I got to my feet again and more carefully inched my way towards the source of the light. When I touched a solid wall the source of light was right in my face. It was a window! Level with my head, and apparently covered with black cloth or paint. I put my face closer and could tell that it had been painted. The glow I had seen was where the paint brush had missed around the edges of the pane.

At first I tried to get my arms high enough behind me to break the glass, but that didn't work. It only reminded me that the butt of an AK47 between my shoulders. had jolted me to the floor. I pondered a few seconds. My groggy brain finally completed the cycle and remembered the box. I probed my way carefully back to the box, remembering that I had tripped over something. I touched the object with my toe. It felt like a sack of potatoes. I stretched my foot over it gingerly and stepped to the other side.

I used my feet to get the box moving toward the window, shuffling it soccer style between them. When I reached the sack of potatoes, I hooked my left foot in the edge of the box and kicked. The box missed the window by three or four feet, and fell noisily to the floor.

Too far away, I thought. I retrieved the box and placed it carefully four feet from the wall, used my roundhouse kick motion and sent it hurtling towards the window. It hit the wall a foot below the window. Too close, I thought. I moved it back again, five feet from the wall. Again I tried the roundhouse motion. Bingo!

The box hit the bottom of the window and glass shattered, suddenly letting in a shaft of muted light. Hoping glass had fallen on the dirt floor, I knelt and felt along the wall with my hands.

My fingers slid over a long sliver of glass and I picked it up gently, placed it on the edge of the box and carefully closed the lid so the glass was wedged between the sides and the lid. I then turned and sat on the box and started sawing on the ropes with the glass.

Minutes later I was free!

I hoped nobody had heard the glass breaking. I stood in one spot, listening for a few minutes. Satisfied that no-one had heard, I picked up the box and ran it around the edge of the window to remove the remaining glass. I stood on the box and managed to get my head and shoulders through the window. After a lot of wiggling and maneuvering I was on the outside of the barn, opposite the house.

I stopped long enough to get my bearings, then ran as fast as my aching hamstrings would let me, back to the bridge. I followed the creek back to the edge of the road and minutes later I was in my Chevy, speeding back up Soledad Canyon Road.

CHAPTER 9

I climbed out of the ruined slacks, tossed them in the trash compactor and turned the hot water on in the tub and let in run while I called Toby. I told him what had happened. He said I would have to come in to the office and file a formal complaint. I had an idea, however, and made another phone call before getting in the tub. I soaked for an hour till the water started to get cold, then took a hot shower, followed by a cold one.

After dressing in Levis and a tee shirt, I opened the closet door and pulled down a box from the top shelf. It contained my old gun that I had bought when I started on the highway patrol. I put the 38 police special in my waistband. These hoods wanted to play rough. I figured I could play rough too.

I drove up the 5 freeway through Hollywood and into the hills. I wanted to see an old friend of mine. She was known as "The Heavenly Hypnotist." Her name was Pat Collette. We had met at a party in Hollywood years ago. I was with a girl that had inspirations to be a popular singer and Pat was there with a stunt man. The stunt man thought all women were the same in Hollywood and wanted to prove it with Pat.

He got real rude, making suggestions and inferences that I thought were out of line. I finally politely told him to shut up. When he got tough with me I used an old Judo trick and slammed him down hard on the floor. The party host and a friend threw the bum out.

Pat was grateful to me. We became friends, eventually lovers. We had kept in touch over the years, sometimes friends, sometimes lovers in a strictly sensual relationship that was mutually satisfactory.

I reached her apartment at about seven and rang the bell. She answered quickly and invited me in.

The apartment was decorated very sparingly. Black velvet couch, chrome, glass-topped coffee table, hardwood floors, no carpet. Modern art pictures on the walls, like science fiction scenes.

Pat was as lovely as usual. She wore a sequined dinner gown, her blond hair piled high on her head, a single string of pearls around her neck. Her breasts were only half covered by the top of the gown, and stuck straight out. We kissed, long and tenderly.

She finally pulled away with a sharp intake of breath.

"I don't have much time, Kip," she breathed heavily, "maybe we should get started."

I thought we had gotten started, and wanted to finish, but then my mind brought back the reason I was there.

"I've heard of cases where people could remember scenes if hypnotized and told that they would remember," I started.

"Kip, baby, if I get you under, I might hypnotize you into staying here till I get back, honey, then give you some post-hypnotic suggestions that would make you do lewd and lascivious acts to me!"

"You don't need hypnosis for that," I laughed. "The fact is, I REALLY need to know if I can remember a license number, then I've got things to do. I wish I could stay, but then a working man has responsibilities..."

"I understand," she said, quickly, "if you promise you'll come back?"

"I promise," I said, crossing my fingers in my pocket.

She asked me some questions about where I had seen the car, what color it was, what I was doing at the time. She then took a single pearl on a gold chain and held it in front of my eyes. She started swinging the pearl and I felt my eyes watching it.

In a soft melodic voice she started talking to me.

"You are in a small, dark room. You are comfortable. You feel tired. Your eyes are burning and you want to close them. Your eyelids are getting heavier, heavier, with each breath you take.

"You are breathing deeply and getting drowsy. The deeper you breath the drowsier you get. The drowsier you get, the deeper you breath. You are drifting off into a deep sleep. I will count to ten and as I count you will get sleepier and sleepier until you are completely asleep.

You will hear everything that I say. You will be asleep but you will be able to talk to me. I am going to start counting now.

One, you are getting sleepier, Two, your hands are heavy; they are hanging at your side and getting heavier. Three, your muscles are relaxing. Four, you feel very comfortable, and relaxed. Five you are drifting into a deep deep sleep. Six, you feel absolutely asleep, completely relaxed. Seven you are sinking deeper and deeper into sleep. Eight, you are drifting on a cloud, sleeping, deep asleep. Nine you are asleep. Ten."

"Kip?" she spoke softly. I could hear the voice but it seemed like it was in a tunnel, echoing inside my head.

"Kip, if you hear me say 'yes'."

"Yes," I said.

"Kip, you are in a dark room. Can you see anything in the room?"

"No, it is dark."

"Is there a window in the room?"

"Yes, but it is closed."

"Open it, Kip."

I opened the window in my mind.

"Is it open now?"

"Yes."

"Look outside, Kip. What do you see?"

"I see a road and some trees."

"Do you see a car?"

"No, but there is a car coming, I hear it!" I could hear the hiss of the tires on the pavement as the big black Cadillac turned off the highway, then the crunch of the heavy car on the rocks, then the silent sound of rubber on asphalt.

"Can you see the car now?"

There it was! It turned the corner and slowed as it passed the spot where my car was hidden. I had a flash of dejevu as though all of this, including the hypnosis had happened before, a weird sensation as though I was asleep and dreaming that I was asleep and dreaming.

"Yes, I see the car."

"Good. Now Kip, what does the car look like?"

I saw the car in my eyes like it was on a television screen. It was long and black. It had the look of a 78 Cadillac limo. I could hear my voice describing the car, telling what I was seeing...the glint of the sun off shiny chrome strips. The dark tinted glass.

"Kip, what is the car doing?"

It is turning, the voice said in my head. It's going up the asphalt road past my car slowly.

"Can you see the back of the car, Kip? Can you see the back of the car now?"

"Yes"

"Look at the license plate, Kip. Can you see it?"

I could see the back of the car plainly. I looked for the license plate in my mind. It was framed in a gold plated frame. There was lettering on the license plate frame that spelled a dealer's name. Roger Penske Cadillac.

"I see it."

"Good, Kip. I want you to tell me the license plate number."

"One, Nine, Eight, Nine."

There was silence. I waited.

"No, Kip, that's the expiration date. What is the license plate number?"

I looked again. There were no numbers. Again I felt disoriented, confused.

"Can you see the numbers, Kip?"

"No!"

"Kip, tell me what you see."

"I see the license plate. It expires One Nine Eight Nine."

"What else is on the license plate?"

"Raingear."

"Raingear? Kip, doe it say Raingear on the license plate?"

"R..A..I..N..G..E..A..R."

"O.K. Kip, you are going to wake up soon. I will count to five. When I reach five you will be fully awake, alert and will not have any thoughts about being asleep. You will remember only the license plate, you will not feel any pain. You will be calm and awake. One, you are starting to wake up now..Two..your eyes are starting to feel good, the burning is gone..you will feel good. Three..you feel normal, relaxed, you are starting to wake up. Four..your eyes are open, you feel awake and relaxed. Five, you are awake."

I woke up. I felt as though I had slept for twelve hours. I felt great. The pain in my shoulder was gone and I had a tremendous feeling of peace and tranquillity.

"Kip?"

"Patty, I feel great. What did you do to me? Make love to me while I was asleep?"

She laughed.

"No, you feel good because you were told that you would. Hypnotism is a very wonderful and powerful tool."

"Raingear!" I said.

"That was what you saw on the license plate, Kip." she said.

"A personalized plate!"

No wonder I had felt confused. There were no numbers on the plate, just letters.

I kissed her. It really felt good. Every muscle in my body was relaxed. As I kissed her, however, one muscle started to constrict. I stepped back and thanked her. We said good-bye at the door and I headed the Chevy back down the Hollywood freeway.

CHAPTER 10

When I reached the interchange I noticed lights flickering off and on behind me and without thinking, pulled to the slow lane to let the car pass. All men are born with some form of ESP. Call it instinct, call it whatever you want. It had saved my life more than once, and it did now.

I glanced to my left and saw the window down on the passenger side of the car. I saw the barrel of a gun.

I reacted as soon as I could. I slammed on the brakes hard. The car on my left roared by just as a shot roared from the gun. A flash leaped toward me from the gun barrel.

I knew instinctively that the car would slow for another shot. I fought the wheel to keep the Chevy under control. A mile back I had passed an exit, Bandini Boulevard.

I cut the wheel hard left and hit the brakes again, this time letting the car slide sideways down the freeway. I held my breath hoping it wouldn't roll. It went up on the right wheels then settled.

I jammed the gear shift lever into reverse and stomped the gas pedal. The car shot backward twenty yards. I braked hard and jerked the lever into low and stomped the gas pedal again. The small engine in the Chevy coughed then caught then screamed as I sped away, up the freeway in the wrong direction, north in the southbound lane.

Fortunately there were few cars. One honked at me frantically as it swerved and missed me.

I glanced in the mirror and saw the taillights of the car carrying my would be killers. They flared bright red and swerved. I swung to my right, to the extreme left lane of the southbound side of the freeway, red lane markers flickering like sparks from a campfire as I flew past them. I slowed and let another car fly past, horn screaming in protest, then cut hard to the left and careened on two wheels around the off ramp.

Off on Bandini, I turned right at the first corner and headed north on Figueroa. When I reached Fourth I cut it hard right again and screamed around the corner. Another right and I was back on the ramp to the southbound freeway. I figured that if my assailants had exited, they wouldn't have time to follow me to this point. If they had not exited, I would be behind them.

Seconds later the dark sedan, horn blaring, roared past me in the wrong direction, north on the freeway. Two men were in the car but I couldn't see their faces. I watched in my mirror as they made the wrong way turn and exited, as I had, off on Bandini. I let out a sigh of relief.

Someone wanted me dead. For now, I was still alive and kicking, maybe not kicking ass, but kicking nonetheless.

My heart slowed gradually to a normal pace and the adrenaline quit squirting into my arteries. I drove south on the Freeway. I felt relatively secure.

There didn't seem to be any way my assailants could have made the guess that I would get right back on the southbound freeway.

To be sure, however, I kept one eye on the road and one on the rearview mirror. Shortly I noticed flashing red lights behind me and eased into the right hand lane to let the emergency vehicle pass. To my surprise the red lights changed lanes too, and as it neared I noticed it was a CHP squad car. I maintained my speed and couldn't believe it when a siren growled behind me and a spot light flicked on and off over my rear window.

I slowed, saw an exit and got off the freeway. I found myself easing to a stop on what used to be Santa Barbara and now is Martin Luther King, Jr. Blvd.

The CHP unit pulled in behind me. I shut off the engine and sat there. Two uniformed highway patrol officers approached, one on my left and one on my right, service revolvers drawn. My brain screamed a warning, but common sense told me to keep still.

A tall, thin highway patrol officer tapped on the driver's side window of my car with the barrel of his gun. I rolled down the window.

"What's the trouble, officer?" I asked.

"Get out of your car with your hands on your head!" the thin man said.

"Sure, but what gives?" I asked, opening the door and easing out with my hands on my head.

He motioned the other office and then holstered his gun and frisked me, running bony fingers down my rib cage, around my waist. He jumped back suddenly when his hand touched the butt of my 38 tucked into my waist.

"He's packing!" he yelled. "Turn around, slowly, and don't twitch!"

I did as I was told. He lifted the 38 out of the waist of my Levis and handed it to the other officer.

"Drop your hands, slowly, and put them behind your back!" he commanded.

"Wait a minute, you guys, I've got a permit for that!"

"Stow it, buddy!" the other officer barked. She was shorter and heavier than the man.

"Cuff him, Terry!" the man said.

She put the cuffs on my wrists and they slammed me into the back seat of the CHP unit. No handles on the inside, no chance to get out.

"What the hell's going on?" I asked.

"You are Kip Yardley ain't you?" the male officer asked.

"Yeah, but if you know that you know I can tote a gun legally. I'm a private investigator working on a murder case. You guys know the rules. I can carry a weapon."

"Having a license to carry and a license to kill are two different things, Yardley," Terry said. She sounded like she was suffering from a severe case of P.M.S.

"WHAT?" I yelled.

"We've got a warrant for your arrest; anything you say may be used against you ....."

"I haven't killed anybody!" I protested. She droned on with the reading of my rights.

I knew it was senseless to argue, so I remained silent till my rights were read then asked,

"Who am I supposed to have bumped?"

"John Doe," skinny said, the term given to a person unknown.

On the way to the county jail they told me that they had checked out my story about being tied and left in a hole under the barn at TARA. When they looked in the hole they found a stiff. He had been shot twice through the heart at close range with a 9mm. Ballistics had ran a check on slugs found at the sight and matched them with the records of my 9mm STAR. It was a perfect match.

I remembered the object that I had stumbled over in the hole. What I thought was a sack of potatoes was a body. A cold shudder passed through me. I had been in that hole with a dead man all that time. Now I was being racked for killing him.

"Toby Smith is a friend of mine," I said. "He will vouch for me. I told him everything I know about the barn."

"We know Smith," Terry said, "If you are friends he'll go your bail, maybe. But for now we've got to take you in."

I kept quiet after that. I knew there was a possibility that Ernesto had shot someone with my gun before he jumped me, but adding anything to my story at this time seemed futile. I figured I'd get a chance to set things straight at the jail.

I was wrong. They gave me the phone call and I called Toby. He promised to get a lawyer and go bail, apologized for putting them on to my car and license plate number, but after all, buddy, I have a job to do, buddy, and your gun fired the rounds that killed John Doe, buddy, and you shoulda stayed on the force, buddy.

"Screw you, buddy," I said, and hung up.

I slept fitfully in the 3 foot by 6-foot bunk in a single cell. At eight the next morning, Freddy France showed up. Freddy was the son of an Air Force Colonel, an "Army Brat" that had never had to do a days work in his life. His sister had married into money and Freddy's life had been one of parties and school. After law school he had set up practice as a defense attorney. Most of his clients were small time hoods, dope pushers and bunco artists, but he believed in the premise that everyone was innocent until proven guilty.

Freddy was in his early thirties, six foot and 195 pounds of tennis playing, suntanned muscle. He was good looking, the suave good looks of a George Hamilton. And cocky. Very Cocky.

"I'll have you out of here before the ink dries on your finger prints," he said, smiling.

Sure, I thought. That would have been hours ago.

"Tell me about your activities yesterday."

I told him the story, starting with my suspicions that my client's brother might have been involved with the shooting of Hoss. I had gone to the Tara ranch to show pictures of Steve Lang to ranch hands to see if anyone recognized him.

I went over the high points, including getting shot at and talking to Ernesto and Hair. I skipped the part about stumbling over the stiff in the hole. No need to play all my cards at once. Besides, that would have placed me at the scene of the crime at the same time the corpse was there. For now, anyway, I didn't want to give them that.

"You'll be out by noon," France said. I shook his hand and he left. I tried to relax on the cot, bones aching from the pounding I had taken. The longer I lay there the madder I got. I needed to be checking things out, like RAINGEAR on a license plate.

I had forgotten to mention that to Toby and cursed at my neglect. Ordinarily I would have thought of that angle, but for some reason had missed it.

After two hours passed I heard the clanging of cell doors and heard my name called. Freddy France apparently had come through. I was out. They handed me my wallet, keys and personal effects. They said I could get my car from the impound lot on Seventh street. Regulations did not permit them to return my gun. I still had my license to carry, but they couldn't give my gun back to me.

Out of the joint, I hailed a cab and had him stop at a pawnshop on Fourth and Soto. I knew the owner, and held a marker. He had been busted for receiving stolen goods and I proved that he was innocent of knowing the goods were stolen.

Now he owed me. After much persuasion and a price that was twice what it was worth, I walked out with a Colt 9mm automatic in my pocket. He was taking a chance, releasing the gun without the waiting period, but I convinced him that I would chew it up and swallow it before I let him get busted for releasing it.

CHAPTER 11

Back at my apartment the first thing I did was pick up the phone and call Toby.

"Toby, you know I didn't ice that guy at TARA."

"I know you didn't, you know you didn't, but the State of California doesn't know you didn't. I was just doing my job, buddy."

"Well, do me a favor then, BUDDY," I shouted the last word, "Run a license number through that computer for me."

"What's up?" he asked. "If you've got something you're not telling me, you could be getting a lot deeper, buddy."

"Right now it's just a hunch, Toby," I said, lightening up on him. "I'll be the first to tell you if I get anything."

"Well, give it to me, then," he said. "I'll run a make on it."

"It's not numbers, actually," I said, "It's one of those personalized plates. A name, maybe. R.A.I.N.G.E.A.R." I spelled it for him.

"O.K.," he said, and I heard the clicking of computer keys. Silence. We waited for the computer to search the files, then I heard Toby mutter under his breath.

"Shoot!"

"What?" I asked.

"You struck out, buddy," he said. "There's no California plate with the letters you gave me.

California plates, as I am reminded by the computer, allow only seven digits or letters. You gave me eight."

"Yeah, why didn't I think of that?" I muttered. Something was wrong. Under hypnosis I had clearly seen a California plate with the word RAINGEAR on it. But California plates do not have eight letters.

"You still there, buddy?" Toby asked.

"Yeah, Toby," I said, quietly. "Thanks anyway." I hung up.

Now what? I asked myself. Back to Pat for some questions.

I picked up the phone again and punched in Pat's number. She answered in a sleepy voice on the third ring.

I hurriedly told her about the computer and the seven-digit rule, and asked her what I had seen while under her spell.

"Hard to say, Kip, darling," she said. "Maybe what you think you saw is actually something that your mind made up, perhaps a word that you thought of at the moment you saw the license plate."

"Under hypnosis you saw the word that you placed in your memory bank, rather than the actual license number."

I was silent for a long time.

"Kip, Darling, you still there?"

"Yeah, I'm here, Pat, just thinking."

"I thought I could hear the wheels turning, Kip. Why not relax for a while? Come on over and let me put you under again. We could have a drink and when you are fully relaxed, we'll try again."

"Sure, Pat," I said, "Thanks."

I knew by the sound of her voice that she had something on her mind besides license plate numbers. We chatted a few minutes. I thanked her again and hung up, after promising to try again.

I had something else I wanted to check out first. If that didn't provide any clues, I would need to relax in any way Pat wanted to.

CHAPTER 12

It was early afternoon when I got in my Chevy and headed for the beach. I knew I was taking a chance trying to talk to the hairy dudes at the beach after our last encounter, but I wanted to try to tie Steve's death to Tara. I was convinced that "Hare" was the ugly bastard that I now had a reason to dislike tremendously. The one who had left me in the hole with a corpse.

As I drove south on the 605 freeway, I thought that perhaps Donna would consent to go to the beach with me and that I wouldn't have to fight my way out of a situation if the beach muscle thought I was a friend of Donna's. I got off the freeway on Katella, the street that leads to Disneyland, and found a phone.

She answered the phone at the Surf Sound office and when she recognized that it was me, her voice changed slightly, to a lower, sexier, sultrier note.

"Sure Kip, I would love to go to the beach with you. I have been so lonely since Steve died, I could cry. I haven't been out of my apartment except to work and school. I feel all tied up in knots inside. Pick me up at 2:30 at my apartment. I'll be waiting. Bye for now," she chattered. It was all one breath.

I was convinced more than ever that the wedding that never was, was never meant to be. The more I knew of this girl, the more it sounded like she would climb into the sack with any guy that paid her any attention at all.

Watch your step, Yardley, I told myself, got back in my car and drove back to the freeway. Traffic was light. I was able to squeeze on with no trouble and took my time driving south with the windows down. I was forced to exit on the southbound 405 when traffic picked up. I sped up a bit, rolled the windows up and turned on the radio.

A local news announcer was rushing through the two o'clock news, and the dull hum of my tires on the highway had me daydreaming until I heard my name.

"A Southland private detective, Kip Yardley, was released from Los Angeles County jail earlier today after being picked up and questioned regarding the finding of a corpse at the Tara ranch, the same ranch where Hoss MacMillan was gunned down last week. Yardley, who served on the California Highway Patrol until 1980 has been released on bail until formal charges are made.."

Just what I need when times are slow, I thought. My name connected with a murder and a tie to Hoss MacMillan. Oh, well, it goes with the territory, I mused.

I flicked the radio to another station and eased down on the gas pedal, urging the old Chevy into a faster lane. At Seal Beach Boulevard I exited from the freeway, wound my way through surface streets and parked in front of Donna's apartment complex. I glanced at my watch and saw that I was early; it was just two o'clock.

I needed to rest so I rolled down the window, put my back to the door and my feet in the seat.

The warm sun was shining through the windshield but my head and shoulders were in the shade of a giant magnolia tree.

I was drifting off to sleep when I heard the shots. My mind was immediately clear, but I reacted slowly. I glanced to my right out the back window of the car, saw nothing.

I turned toward the passenger's window. Out of the corner of my eye I saw a man in Levis and a tee shirt running down the sidewalk away from Donna's door. He didn't see me slumped in my car. He turned right and ran down the street towards the ocean, head down, at full speed. I thought I saw the handle of a gun sticking in the waistband of his Levis. I got a good look at his face, but didn't recognize him. He wore dark sunglasses. His hair was long and he had a beard. His legs were long and lanky.

I jerked the glove compartment door open and grabbed the Colt, opening the car door as I did. I stumbled out of the car, almost fell, caught my balance and sprinted after the tall man. He was a good forty yards away. As we ran a light colored pickup truck pulled to the curb ahead of him. He hurdled the sides of the truck in one leap and the truck roared away, screeching tires and whining engine.

I stopped, pocketed the Colt and ran back to the entrance of Donna's apartments. I could hear sirens starting to moan in the background somewhere.

I didn't know which apartment Donna occupied, but as I ran the nosy landlady came running out of the open door, one hand on her mouth, the other gesturing behind her at an open door. I ran in.

The long hallway lead straight from the door and I could see a door open on my left. I turned the corner into the room, sliding sideways on the carpet.

She lay on her back on the floor in front of a white couch. A dark stain was spreading slowly on the white carpet under her chest. Two neat, round holes in her chest, right between her bare breasts. Her eyes were glazed.

The telephone lay swinging from its cord.

I knelt beside her and touched her wrist feeling for a pulse. There was a faint smell of gunpowder in the air. No pulse. I put my ear next to her mouth to listen for breath. She muttered one word. Hair.

Then she died.

The sirens were getting closer. I knew there was no time for me to do any explaining. I'd be back in the pokey for sure. Something told me to run.

I sprinted out the back and glanced to the left, down an alley. I ran down the alley hearing car tires screeching in front. I vaulted a low fence and sprinted fifty yards down a side street to a corner gas station, where I slowed to a walk.

I went into the men's room at the gas station and locked the door behind me. I waited.

I had to count on the frightened landlady not being able to recognize me and remember my name. I waited until I thought it was safe, then left the restroom.

Ambling up the street like a tourist I turned the corner and saw three policemen standing in front of

Donna's apartment. A paramedic was kneeling over a prone landlady.

I walked slowly to my car, got in and started the engine. I noticed that the keys were still in the ignition and the radio was on. Country music wafted softly to the branches of the magnolia tree.

A cop glanced at me as the car started, but turned his back on me immediately. So far, so good. I put the car in gear and edged away from the curb. Glancing to my right I saw the landlady sit up suddenly and stare right at my car.

I goosed the accelerator slightly and the old Chevy responded with a sudden acceleration. A glance in the rear view mirror told me the cops with the landlady were starting to get curious about me.

By the time I reached Pacific Coast Highway I was sure that they were going to come after me. I made a fast right and slipped into traffic, all the while keeping one eye on the rear view mirror.

When I reached the first intersection, I knew I was home free. No sirens. I relaxed a little and tried to think of what my next move would be. I decided now, more than ever, I needed to talk with the muscle brains at the beach. A little maneuvering on side streets put me on Second Street in Long Beach, headed towards the Plunge.

If those goons knew about Hare, and from the reactions at our first meeting, they did, then I wanted to discuss Donna with them.

I decided that from this point on I was going to play a little tougher game.

CHAPTER 13

I parked the car and walked quickly to the edge of the sand and glanced toward the volleyball courts. No one there. I walked across the sand until I could see beyond the concrete wall. The beach was nearly deserted, but to my right, thirty feet away sat the dark-haired girl who had been the recipient of my card. Bingo, I said to myself.

Approaching her slowly, I stopped when my shadow fell across the magazine she was reading. She raised her head and glanced at me.

"Move it, Creep!" she said.

"Look, I'm sorry I beat up on your boyfriends," I said, shifting so that my shadow no longer fell on her magazine. "They started it, though. I just wanted to ask a couple of questions."

"We don't like nosy people around here," she said.

"A guy named Steve is dead," I said, and let it soak in, watching for reactions.

"Damn you!" she said and suddenly started crying. Huge, uncontrollable sobs racked her shoulders.

If there's one thing I can't stand it's seeing a woman cry.

I sat on the edge of her towel and waited for the sobbing to stop. When she reached in her purse for a tissue, I glanced at her.

"I'm sorry," I said, and meant it. "I was hired to find his killer. I didn't realize you were that close a friend. Sorry."

"We used to go together before Donna," she said, sniffling.

"Donna is dead too," I said, watching her face.

"What?? When??.." she stammered.

I told her what I had just seen. She started to cry again. I waited patiently until her sobbing stopped, gently placed my hands on her bare shoulders and turned her to face me.

"This is not a kid's game," I told her. "Some of your friends play for keeps, and the stakes are getting higher."

"What do you mean?" she asked, stuttering.

"Apparently Steve did something that Donna knew about. Someone wanted to make sure that whatever she knew she didn't tell."

I let her think about that for a few minutes. She tried to pull herself together, but occasionally her shoulders would heave and a sob would escape like a quail before a hunter.

"Look, I don't even know your name," I said, "but whatever you know about Hare, and Steve, could be enough to make someone want you dead, too."

Suddenly her whole body shook violently and she buried her head on my shoulder and the sobbing started in earnest. She was really shaken up and I felt that if I didn't get her under control she was going to freak out on me.

I cradled her in my arms, picked her up, stooped and got her purse and a corner of the towel. I walked slowly back to my car. Once there I sat her down, opened the door and eased her in.

"Where are you taking me?" she asked between sobs.

"To a friend's house," I said. "You'll be safe there for a few days till this mess blows over."

"But I'll need some clothes and my makeup and stuff," she protested.

"We'll stop at your place and get some. Where do you live?"

"I live with Donna," she said, "I mean, I DID live with.." she started crying again.

"Well, that's out," I said. "I can't take you there."

My idea had been to take her to Toby's place for a few days till I was sure she didn't know anything that would get her killed. Toby's wife was understanding as hell. I figured she would get the girl under control.

Now, I didn't know. She did need clothes, all she had with her was a robe and a bikini. She needed makeup too. All the crying had smeared her eye shadow. She looked like a sick calf. A cute sick calf.

"I have an idea," I said. "Do you know Steve's sister, Starla?"

"I met her once."

"I'll take you there. You'll be safe there, and she will let you borrow some of her clothes. You two are about the same size."

I fumbled in the glove compartment for my beat up notebook and thumbed it open to Starla's name. I memorized the address and put the book away.

"I don't even know your name," I said.

"It's Carol. Carol Bellew," she said.

I tried to spell it, got it right on the third try.

"I'm Kip Yardley." I smiled.

"I know," she said. "You gave me your card, remember?"

"Oh yeah," I said, blushing. "I meant that for the benefit of your muscle bound buddies."

"You mean Gary and Bill."

"Is that their names?"

"The big one that you put down first was Gary," she said.

"Have you talked to either of them about Steve's death?" I asked.

"Well, we talked about it," she said. "Steve played volleyball a lot with the guys, and we drank beer and partied together."

"Did Steve ever mention making a lot of money?"

"Steve was always talking about making a lot of money," she said. "He was a schemer and a dreamer. Most of his ideas were too wild to pay any attention to. The last one especially."

My ears perked up.

"What was the last one?" I asked, breathing faster.

"He was going to sell a lotta weed, make a bundle. Him and Donna were gonna get married."

"Did Donna know that was his plan?"

"I don't know, she never talked much about it. I knew from talking to the guys."

"How much is a lot?" I asked.

"I don't know how much marijuana. He just mentioned two hundred and fifty thousand dollars."

"That's a lotta weed," I said.

"He claimed that he had it. Said he was waiting on a guy to come up with the money."

"Did he mention the guys name?"

"Yeah, it was Hair. That's why we didn't want to talk to you. We thought you might be one of the people responsible for Steve's death."

The apartment Starla lived in was an older building, an "L" shaped, two-story stucco, painted white with blue trim. A sparkling pool sat in the middle of the courtyard, surrounded by a walkway. Between the walkway and the building, twisted junipers and philodendrons graced the landscape.

We climbed the stairs at one end of the building and walked the upstairs deck to Starla's apartment and rang the bell.

I heard footsteps inside the apartment. Good, Starla was home.

The door swung open. Starla looked startled to see me.

"Mr. Yardley," she said.

"Starla, I need to ask a favor," I started.

"Come in," Starla held the door open and stood aside, waiting for us to come in.

We went in. The apartment was not well decorated, flowery design on a sectional, plum colored carpets, lime green walls with modern distasteful pictures.

"Do you know Carol?" I asked

"We've met." Starla said, a hidden something in her voice. I didn't think it was dislike, it just sounded strange, suppressed.

"Hi, Starla," Carol said.

"I have some shocking news, Starla," I said, "Perhaps you should have a seat, and I'll bring you up to date as easy as I can."

"What is it?" she asked, a startled look springing to her eyes.

"Please, sit down," I said.

She sat on the couch and motioned us to set down. Carol sank into an overstuffed chair, and I sat on the edge of the couch.

"Donna is dead," I said.

Her disbelief was equal to that which Carol had shown earlier. She wanted to know the details, but did not fall to pieces. Her demeanor was simply one of disbelief.

I started at the beginning with my trip to the beach, my fight with Gary and Bill, the trip to Tara. I didn't leave out anything, and when I told them of my arrest they wanted to know why. Apparently they hadn't been watching the news.

I told them about the corpse at Tara.

Carol started to reel around in the chair and her face turned ashen gray instantly.

"Carol, what's the matter?" I asked, "You look like you're going to faint."

"Gary went to Tara to see Hare!" she sighed.

The two girls stared blankly at each other, then at me. I felt stupid. A sickening feeling spread through my stomach as I realized who the stiff was in the hole at TARA.

I tried lamely to apologize, mumbling and stammering words about getting people involved in things that I shouldn't have, asking the wrong people questions. I stammered on till Starla stopped me.

"Don't be silly, Kip," she said. "None of this is your fault."

We talked for a while; I brought Starla up to date on the conversation Carol and I had.

Starla was shocked to hear that Steve had planned to sell a large amount of marijuana.

"Steve had found a source for some grass, and was willing to sell it to Hare for 250 grand," I mused. "That's still a lot of grass to come up with. Any idea where he was going to get it?"

Starla looked at me with a blank look.

Carol sighed again.

"He just said he could get his hands on it whenever he wanted to, that's all," she said, frowning. "I guess that meant that he already had it, but that it was stored somewhere."

"That's a thought," I said.

My mind was racing ahead. High quality Marijuana would bring about $20 an ounce. Roughly that would be 780 pounds of pot. A sizable lot, requiring a large storage area.

"Maybe he rented a space somewhere," Starla said. "I don't know. He never mentioned any of this to me."

"Gary and Bill weren't convinced he had it," Carol said. "He was always talking about big deals and things he wanted to do."

"One last question, Carol," I said. "And this may hurt. You said you used to go with Steve. What happened to make you break up."

"Well, it wasn't like we were engaged or anything," she replied. "I met Steve on the beach and we went out a couple of times. Then I met Gary and started going with him. Steve starting going with Donna. He told me once that she could be a real asset to his ambition if things didn't go right with the pot sale."

"Did he elaborate on that?" I asked.

"No, just that she was in a position to do someone a lot of harm."

I asked to use Starla's phone and called Toby. He advised me to come to the station and make a statement about being at Donna's. I declined.

I told him I was not going to be tossed in jail twice in the same day for something I didn't do, but was keeping my promise to inform him of what I was finding in my investigation.

Some things I feel cops are better off not knowing till all of the chips are down. I declined to tell Toby about Steve's plan to sell a large amount of marijuana.

I hung up and said good-bye to the girls, promising to call later and let them know my progress. Now I was investigating four deaths, Hoss MacMillan, Steve Lang, Donna and Gary. I wondered, briefly, how I let myself get messed up in these cases. Money, I told myself.

I headed the Chevy for my apartment. I needed to think and the best place I could think of to relax and let my mind wander was home.

In the shower, in the pool, or on the couch, I think better at home.

At the apartment, I let myself in, grabbed a beer from the fridge and stretched out on the couch. I flicked on the news and watched as a solemn newscaster told of yet another shooting, this time a young reporter for a Seal Beach weekly newspaper.

I knew the facts better than they did so I flicked to another channel and watched in disgust as the Dodgers lost another spring training game to the Mets. Lasorda, I thought, couldn't manage his way out of a wet paper sack.

I let myself relax and used my meditation technique to blank my mind. The technique had been a blessing after my divorce. It kept me from going crazy or becoming an alcoholic. I thought about the kids.

It's one thing to walk away from a woman who no longer loves you and quite a different thing to walk away from four little children who adore you, and for whom you would gladly lay down your life.

The only problem was, I had learned the technique a little late. After my divorce, the first thing I learned was that contrary to my first wife's opinion, I am not a lousy lover. The second thing I learned is that I am not cut out to be alone. I need a woman around me. Maybe not all the time, but I need companionship, and sex. Not always the sex, but always the companionship.

And I need my children.

My ex wife had tried to use the children as bargaining chips. If I was a good little boy and paid my child support on time, became a hermit, never called to ask about the kids, then I could have my visitation rights.

But if I went out with other women, tried to see the kids at anytime other than visitation, she punished me by refusing to let me see them.

One time a live-in friend of hers had told me I couldn't see my children when I showed up on visitation day. I almost killed him.

I was sound asleep when the phone aroused me from a dream. In my dream I HAD killed the bastard and five thousand cops were chasing me through the streets of Los Angeles.

"Kip, Darling," the voice murmured after I muttered hello.

"Oh, if it isn't my favorite stiff drink serving, rubberdowner." I said.

"What?" she laughed.

"Oh nothing, Miss Collette," I said. "Just thinking."

"Well, come on over and let me fix you a drink and give your hard body a rubdown," she purred. Not only is she a hypnotist, she reads minds as well.

"I cant right now, Pat," I said. "There's something I need to check out first. Keep the lid on the bourbon for me."

CHAPTER 14

Friday morning.

Steve Lang's place turned out to be a Spanish style bungalow house with a flat roof and a row of red tile around the top. The lawn was cemented in right up to a low wall next to the front sidewalk. A table sat on the cement with a large umbrella shading it. The black umbrella had PERRIER written in gold letters around it, and beneath it sat a uniformed police officer reading a newspaper.

The policeman was from the Long Beach department and I recognized him. He was the son of an old friend of mine that I had known while on the highway patrol. His dad was now retired, but had been a Long Beach homicide detective.

I hoped the cop wouldn't recognize me as I parked the Chevy at the curb and got out. I decided to play it dumb.

"Hello, Officer," I said, smiling.

He glanced up, squinted, then pulled his visor down to shade his eyes. I don't think he recognized me.

"What can I do for you, sir?"

"I'm with Prudent Forester Insurance," I lied. "I am trying to get in touch with a Steve Lang regarding his auto insurance policy."

"You can cancel that policy, mister," he drawled, "Mister Lang is no longer in the land of the living. He was shot three days ago."

"No!" I said, showing as much shock as I could muster. "You don't say. I just talked to him a few days ago regarding his insurance policy."

"Well, he won't be needing it."

"Say, I wonder, is his wife home? Maybe I could talk to her about the policy."

"He wasn't married, bub," he said. "Not only that but his girl friend was shot yesterday. She's dead too."

"Well, that does it, I guess," I said and got back in my car.

I drove around the block and parked on the next street. The house directly behind Lang's was a two-story conversion, like many houses in the beach area. I watched the front of it for a few minutes, trying to determine if anyone would see me go through the yard to the back. I could see no life, but just to be sure I opened the glove box and pulled out a cardboard box.

Shuffling through the box, I came up with a dozen or so badges and pulled out the one I was looking for. SOUTHERN COUNTIES GAS COMPANY. I pinned on the badge, picked up a clipboard from the back seat and headed for the house.

So far, so good, I thought.

As I rounded the edge of the house I almost walked off into the deep end of a swimming pool. The pool took the entire back yard except for a walkway around it. I edged my way around the pool and to the fence separating it from the Lang house. No one stopped me, and as I glanced around, I saw that the diving board was near the fence.

I stepped to the board and with a slight jump grabbed the top of the block fence, swung my legs up and dropped silently into the yard behind it.

I crouched and ran to the rear of Lang's house, squeezing behind a Cypress tree next to a window. Satisfied that I was undetected, I tried the window and found that it was unlocked. Luck!

The window came open without a sound and I hoisted myself up, dropped hands and head first into a room. It turned out to be a small hallway off the kitchen. I left the window open and silently crept around a wall, looking for a window where the cop out in front might see me.

Assured that I wouldn't be spotted, I walked through the house until I found a bedroom. The house was small, and I guessed that there would be only two bedrooms. The first one I entered had not been used to sleep in. It was filled with weight lifting equipment. One wall was covered with mirror tiles. I eased back to the hall and took the other door. It swung open and I stepped through into Steve Lang's bedroom.

The cops had been there before me; it was evident. Things had been moved, drawers opened, and shuffled through. Socks rolled into tight little balls were carelessly dropped on the floor. Underwear and tee shirts hung half out of the dresser drawers.

I eased each drawer out as far as it would go and felt under it. Cops do not search in places that I do.

They have a mentality that differs from that of a private investigator's. They look for obvious things, guns, drugs or drug paraphernalia, but do not search for other things that the subject might purposefully be trying to conceal.

Satisfied there were no false bottom drawers or envelopes taped beneath them, I made my way to the closet. Clothes hung neatly on plastic hangers, mostly casual clothes with a couple of suits. Shirts were hung on one side, slacks on the other. A dozen pair of shoes sat neatly in plastic stacked boxes.

I felt in the toes of the shoes. The third pair I picked up had an envelope rolled and stuffed in the toes. I opened it and removed a stack of pictures.

In the dim light of the bedroom I made out that the pictures were of something stored in what appeared to be burlap bags. Two policemen and two plain-clothed men smiled at the camera. I tucked the pictures back in the envelope and stuffed it in the rear pocket of my jeans.

I didn't know what it meant, but I had the uncanny feeling that I had found the reason for Steve Lang's death.

Through the years I have developed intuition that borders on what some might call extra sensory perception. Something tells me when I am on to something important, and these pictures were screaming at me in loud voices, "IMPORTANT, IMPORTANT."

I continued my search, finding nothing else in the bedroom. I left the bedroom and made my way back to the bathroom and removed the cover on the toilet tank and looked inside. Nothing. I really hadn't expected to find anything there. Most cops will look there for drugs.

I carefully opened the medicine cabinet and as I did I thought about an old Candid Camera television show where medicine cabinets were filled with marbles to catch snoopy people. Fortunately this one wasn't booby-trapped that way.

It held the usual: toothpaste, toothbrush a few bottles of after-shave lotion and a half empty bottle of mouthwash. There was only one glass shelf in it, and I wasted little time removing all of the items and the shelf.

With a small screwdriver that I carry on my key chain, I removed the two screws that held the medicine cabinet to the wall. They came out very easily. I grabbed the edges with both hands and gently removed it from the drywall, pulling straight out. It came out silently and easily.

There was a nail driven into the side of the two-by-four in the cavity where the cabinet had been. A string was attached to the nail. I lifted the string. The short length was looped around a plastic bag the size of a large freezer bag. Something inside the bag was wrapped in old newspapers.

I untied the knot, unrolled the bag and gently lifted the package out. The old newspapers were not that old. One of them was dated the day before Steve Lang died.

I unrolled the newspaper. Inside was marijuana. I weighed the package in my hand and mentally calculated that it was about two pounds of tightly compressed marijuana. I started to rewrap the compressed marijuana when something in the paper caught my eye.

The headlines were "SHERIFFS BUST POT GANG" and there was a picture of a group of men, some uniformed some in plain clothes.

Just as I started to read the article, I heard the front door open and a footstep in the house.

I jammed newspaper and marijuana in the plastic bag and up under my shirt, left the medicine cabinet sitting on the edge of the sink and stepped quietly out of the bathroom. I could hear the footsteps walking toward the kitchen.

Quickly, I entered the hall off the kitchen, stepped through the window and pulled my torso through. I knew if I dropped I might scrape against the house and make a noise, but I also knew that anyone entering the kitchen could see my left leg sticking out behind me in the hall. I took a chance and pushed away from the house with both hands and dropped with a roll onto the lawn.

With two long strides, I reached the wall and leaped for the top. I swung my legs up, scrambled to the top and vaulted over it to the other side.

What I forgot was the pool.

The cold surface of the pool surged over me with a splash that sent ripples of water out on the other side. When my head came back to the surface, I gasped and kicked out for the side of the pool.

Pulling myself up on the pool ladder, I saw a very nice pair of legs. As I continued up the ladder and my eyes climbed higher I found myself looking at a very nice woman.

She was tall, maybe five-nine, well tanned, and muscular, like she might be one of those women who work out with weights, or one who swims a lot. Dark eyes, dark hair. A beautiful smile showed perfectly even white teeth. The kind of teeth you see in toothpaste commercials. She was not a beautiful girl, but not very far from it.

"What are you doing in my pool?" she asked.

"I, I, uh, uh..," was all I could say.

"Spit it out!" she demanded.

"I don't have it in my mouth," I said. "I'm afraid I swallowed half of it."

"You know what I mean," she grinned. "Just tell me."

"I accidentally fell in," I said.

"What are you doing in my back yard then?" she wanted to know.

"I was reading your meter," I lied.

I thumbed at the badge that I had pinned to the pocket of my shirt.

"Oh!" she said.

"Well, I'm sorry I fell in your pool," I said, shivering.

"Oh, that's all right. You're not hurt are you?"

"I don't think so."

"Well you're shivering like a dog. Why don't you come in and dry off before you catch your death of cold?" she smiled.

"I'd better keep on going on my route," I said. The wet marijuana was starting to give off the particular odor that only marijuana has.

"Are you sure?" she asked, smiling that lovely toothpaste smile.

I wasn't sure, and as I glanced toward the rear fence, I wondered if whoever had came into Steve Lang's house was listening. I needed to get out of this mess fast.

The girl was tempting me with her eyes and her smile. I could see that she might be offering more than a dry towel, but the urgency of the situation meant playing it cool.

"I'm pretty sure," I smiled back.

"My name is Rhonda," she said, and extended a hand with long fingers and long shiny nails. "Rhonda Rhodes."

"I'm Bob," I lied, shaking her hand gently.

"Well, Bob, it's nice to meet you. I would rather have met you with dry clothes on, not that my clothes are wet, but yours certainly are, and I think I could get to know you quite well if I had met you with some dry clothes on, not that mine are wet."

"No, they aren't wet," I agreed. "Mine are."

We stood there looking at each other sheepishly for a second, then both of us laughed.

"Can we talk about this some other time?" I asked.

"Sure," she said. "You know where I live. Come back any time."

I promised her that I would.

I listened again for any sign that the person in Steve Lang's house had heard the commotion here. The only sound I heard was the closing of the window that I had opened, and the young cop muttering to himself about homicide leaving windows open.

I told her how nice it was to have met her.

"I would like very much to swim in your pool without my clothes on," I said, then thinking of how that sounded, I apologized and said with maybe a bathing suit on, and she said, she knew what I meant. She looked at me with those very pretty large brown eyes and grinned.

I left. I had to leave, because things could have easily gotten completely out of hand had I stayed.

CHAPTER 15

I stayed off of the main highways, drove slowly and deliberately back to my apartment. When I reached the neighborhood, I cruised around the block twice, looking for unmarked police cars. I didn't need any cops asking questions about two pounds of marijuana and wet clothes.

Convinced there were no cops around, I parked my car in the carport and made my way to the apartment.

I let myself in, locked the dead bolt behind me and withdrew the package from under my shirt. The marijuana had stained the front of my white tee shirt, and the ink from the newspaper had smudged all over the front of my chest. I smelled like an alfalfa field after a rainstorm.

I spread the paper out on the small kitchen table to dry, stuck the wet marijuana in the freezer compartment of the refrigerator and stepped into the bathroom for a shower.

Ten minutes later I had the pictures from my back pocket and the newspaper carefully laid out side by side.

The article in the newspaper was about Los Angeles County Sheriff Thad Yates seizing a marijuana cache. The pictures were of Yates and the mayor and a couple of policemen, standing next to bales of marijuana.

Thad Yates, who announced yesterday that he is a candidate for governor of California, has once again intercepted a major drug shipment that would have wound up in the streets of our city.... The article said....

With a street value of over two million dollars, this is the second largest marijuana find in Los Angeles County history, and the third this month for Yates and his deputies.... The article said.

I started to put the paper and the pictures away when I noticed something unusual about the photos. The bundles of marijuana were stacked slightly higher than Yates' head. On the top row of bundles, second from the end were some very faint letters of some sort.

I found a magnifying glass in my desk drawer and looked at the letters closely.

SLDW. The newspaper photos differed.

At first the letters meant nothing to me. I sat there a minute or two, got a cup of coffee and made myself a peanut butter and jelly sandwich. Nibbling on the sandwich, I couldn't shake the feeling I had experienced when I found the photos at Steve Lang's house.

Steve Lang!

"S" "L" and the "D" "W" was Donna Wilson!

I was on to something. I didn't have the foggiest idea why Steve Lang would take a marking pencil and write his and Donna's initials on a bag of marijuana. I was as certain that he had as I was certain that Rhonda wanted me to swim in her pool without my clothes on.

I nibbled on my sandwich and sipped my coffee while I ran back over the entire case. I flipped the pages in my mind like I was reading a book, carefully reading each step, trying not to miss a single word. I looked for clues and meanings and tried to piece the puzzle together. Nothing jumped off the pages of my mind. I was drawing a complete blank.

The phone startled me out of my concentration.

I grabbed it and answered on the second ring.

"Kip, ol' buddy!"

"Toby," I said.

"Where the hell have you been, Kip? I've been looking for ya and looking for ya!"

"You wouldn't believe me if I told you, Toby," I said.

"Try me, buddy."

"Well, I went for a swim," I said, truthfully.

"Oh, come on, Kip," Toby whined, "I want to know what you know about Donna Wilson's death."

"I know very little," I lied.

"Bring me up to date, Kip"

I told him about trying to talk to Donna, about the man I had seen running from her place and about finding her dead. I didn't tell him about the trip to Steve Lang's house. No need to give him something that I couldn't figure out until it meant something to me.

"We figured you were there," he said. "The landlady thought she had seen you before, said you had been there a few days ago looking for Donna."

"Yep!"

"Well, I just wanted you to know that we need to keep in touch, Kip. I can't keep the state of California off your ass. I've got a job to do, and you know how I feel about my job."

"Yep," I said again, and hung up on him.

CHAPTER 16

Saturday morning. I had to find out why a man who had been shot down on the Long Beach freeway would have pictures of the County Sheriff and two pounds of marijuana hidden behind a medicine cabinet.

When you want to question the fox, you go to the fox den.

Los Angeles County Sheriff Thad Yates had been elected to office in 1950 and reelected in every election year since then. He was a people's choice type of sheriff, hard on criminals, hard on drugs and very right wing politically. He was a favorite with the L. A. police department and buddy-buddy with the Chief of Police, Billy Bob Dalton.

The two were like Siamese twins, joined at the brain. They had very little use for anyone other than Anglo-Saxon Protestant men. They controlled their departments like kings rather than elected officials, promoting those who agreed politically and surrounding themselves with power. Only the Hollywood Democrats were untouchable, and only then because of the money they could throw around.

It was almost like the early fifties: the power and control over who worked in Hollywood depended on how far to the left they leaned.

Thad Yates was a Reagan-Bush supporter who believed the only good Democrat was a Hollywood producer or director.

I had to go through a few friends on the Highway Patrol to find out Yates' address. He lived in the Alhambra district, high on a hill and a stone's throw from the San Gabriel River.

The house was white, surrounded with sago palms, eucalyptus and yucca trees. Arched doorways and arched windows reflected the Spanish influence. Oleander bushes were delicately placed in proper landscape spots and the smell of their blossoms permeated the morning air.

Nearly as powerful was the smell of chlorine from an Olympic size pool at the side of the house. Tennis courts lined three sides of the pool area and another white stucco building nestled on the side of a hill at the rear of the two-acre lot. A guesthouse, I thought.

I used a mental calculator and appraised the value of the place like a real estate agent had taught me to do. It figured at about $750 thousand. Not bad for an elected official whose salary was supposed to be $85 thousand a year.

It was Saturday morning, and I hoped to catch Yates at home. As I approached the front door, heels clicking on glazed Mexican tiles, I was curious, but apprehensive, about what Yates might know regarding the pictures. I had to find a way to ask the right questions without giving away how I obtained the pictures.

The door chimes rang hollow through the spacious entry and a young man opened the door.

He looked to be perhaps twenty years of age. His curly hair was combed straight back. It was black as coal and his eyebrows were thick and just as dark. He smiled, showing perfect white teeth.

"Good morning, sir," he said, appraising my six foot frame with dark twinkling eyes. "May I help you?"

"Morning," I said. "I would like to speak with Sheriff Yates. Is he in?"

"And who shall I tell the sheriff is calling?" he asked.

"Just tell him a former Highway Patrol officer," I said.

If he were told that a private detective wanted to see him, he would find a reason not to be available, but a former Highway Patrol officer could be anyone.

"Right away, sir," the young man said. He turned and disappeared into the house, leaving me standing at the huge oak door thinking that I would not want a butler like this one.

Not that I have anything against any particular lifestyle, but this guy was as queer as a three dollar bill.

I hummed an old tune in my mind. I'm looking over a four-leaf clover that I've overlooked before. I changed the words slightly. I'm looking over a three-dollar bill that I've never seen before.

Twinkle Toes soon came back and ushered me in.

The entry hall was as big as my apartment. Marble tile glistened under my feet. Gold edged mirrors hung floor to ceiling. A chandelier glistened high over my head.

The vaulted ceilings made the room look cavernous. I followed Twinkle Toes across the tiled entry and down three steps to a carpeted living room big enough to play football in.

Sitting in a white leather recliner reading a paper was Thad Yates.

He dropped the paper on the floor next to the chair and looked up at me.

"I'm Thad Yates," he said in that self-important way that makes me want to puke.

Some men are so full of their own importance that whenever they open their mouths, it rolls out with their voices. His voice was soft and deep, like it came from the bottom of a well.

"Mr. Yates, my name is Yardley," I said. "Kip Yardley. I'm a private detective."

His eyebrows arched and he gave Twinkle Toes a curious glance and then looked back at me.

"And what brings you here, Mr. Yardley?" he asked.

"I'm investigating a murder that occurred on the Long Beach Freeway near San Pedro," I said.

"I'm afraid you have the wrong department, Yardley," he said and lowered his legs so the recliner snapped shut with a schussing noise.

"You probably should be talking to the Highway Patrol."

Again his eyes flicked towards Twinkle Toes and his eyebrows arched slightly.

"I believe they are investigating too, sir," I said.

"What I am interested in is a story that was printed a few weeks ago in the Times, the one where your people made the big Marijuana bust?" I ended it with a question in my voice.

"What about it?" he asked, rising from the chair. "Can I get you a drink, Yardley?"

"No thank you, I never drink before ten," I lied.

"What about the drug bust?" he asked.

"Well I'm curious as to why the letters SLDW would appear on one of the bales of marijuana," I said. I watched his eyes for any sign that he might know about those letters.

"And you think I would know?" he asked.

"It occurred to me that you would be the man to ask," I said. "You are in the pictures along with the bales of marijuana..those initials are on one of the bales. I thought you might know why."

"I can assure you, Yardley," he smiled, "I don't know what the hell you are talking about."

I reached into my inside jacket pocket and carefully extracted one of the photos. I showed it to him. He took it and held it out at arm's length like a man who normally needs reading glasses.

"I don't see what you are talking about either," he said.

I pointed to the little black smudged letters on the bale next to his head and handed him my magnifying glass.

He looked through the glass, muttered under his breath, "SLDW".

"S.L.D.W.," I repeated. "Steve Lang, Donna Wilson."

"I see," he said, and returned the magnifying glass and paper to me.

"Does it mean anything to you?"

"Not a thing, Yardley," he said. "Should it?"

"Well, Steve Lang and Donna Wilson are both dead. Shot dead," I said.

"I heard about that," he said, no trace of anything in his voice.

"Is it possible that Lang could have marked these bags because he intended to steal some of the marijuana?" I asked. "He was employed by the highway department. I understand you used highway department personnel to move the seized marijuana to county custody."

"Well, anything is possible," he said, pouring a drink from a glass decanter. He replaced the bottle on the foldout bar next to a huge fireplace.

"What's this got to do with me, Yardley?"

"I'm not sure, Sir," I answered truthfully.

"I'm sorry I can't be of more help to you then," he said. "Show Mr. Yardley out, Chico."

Chico took my arm. I pulled it away, not fast, just firmly so that Chico, alias Twinkle Toes, would know I don't like men putting their hands on me.

He looked at me with a hurt expression in his eyes.

"Right this way, Sir."

"Thanks for your time," I told Yates, and left.

CHAPTER 17

My Chevy was hot even though I had parked it on the shady side of the street. I rolled down the window on the driver's side before I got in and then slammed the door, cranked the key in the ignition and drove away. I was mad as hell.

I had an eerie feeling that Yates knew about those letters on the bale before I showed him the picture. And I had another eerie feeling that Mister Right Wing Big Shot Sheriff was a homosexual.

Not that I give a damn about people's lifestyles. I just can't stand hypocrites. For years the Sheriff's department had taken a hard line about homosexuals on the police forces. Applicants had to sign sworn documents that they were not, nor had ever been homosexual. And here the top dog in the department was either entertaining a gay houseguest or had hired a gay housekeeper. Something was rotten in Denmark.

Shades of J. Edgar Hoover, I thought, as I drove back toward my apartment.

Nothing had come of the trip to see Yates, and I was disappointed. I had expected something, even though I didn't have the slightest idea what it was. But the results were zip. Nada. Zero. Naught. The more I thought about the way this case was going, the madder I got. I decided to head for the Zansabuku and have a cold beer and relax. Things have a way of getting to me after a while when I can't seem to make any progress on a case, and this was one of those times.

At the bar I parked in the rear, stuck my head through the door to make sure Maria was nowhere around, and sauntered in. Jim was off duty, and I didn't know the bartender.

I ordered a bottle of Miller Lite and poured it into a frosted glass. It was only 10:30 in the morning but the beer tasted good.

I watched a tennis match on the television above the bar, only half paying attention to it. The anger over the way things had gone in the past few days was building.

I paid for the beer, got in the car and headed for Garden Grove. I needed to talk to Toby again about the license plate letters. I was starting to feel sure that the damned car had contained either Ernesto or Hair, or both, and I had a score to settle with those two.

In the CHP office, I asked a clerk if Toby was in and was told that he would be off for the weekend. Disgusted, I got back in the Chevy and headed for Tara. I would be more careful this time and not let myself get tossed in a hole under a barn.

The sun was out and starting to get hot, but a bank of dark clouds was settling in across the western skies. I figured it would rain before sunset.

On the Lancaster freeway, headed for Soledad Canyon Road, I started to wonder just what the hell I was doing on this case. I had been shot at, beat up, shot at again, tossed in jail and damned near drowned in a swimming pool while fully clothed.

One thing is for sure. I am not a quitter. I don't enjoy every case I get. But I stick to them.

Once I had spent three weeks trying to find the heir to a million and a half dollars. The last known address I had on the guy turned out to be 16 years old. I waded through run down neighborhoods in the worst parts of town, seedy flop joints, stinky bars and in and out of a hundred little machine shops trying to find the guy.

When I finally found him and told him that he had inherited a million and a half dollars, he didn't even thank me.

I didn't expect a huge tip. I didn't expect any tip, but I did expect a thank you.

This case had a pot of gold at the end of the rainbow. I figured I would at least get a dinner date with Starla Lang. Might even get further than that. And if all else failed, I could call Rhonda. Tall, lanky, good-looking Rhonda. She had a wicked smile that was teasing my imagination when I thought about it.

I drove past the entrance to Tara and up the lane where I had parked the Chevy on my previous visit. Further up I passed a small cross street with the typical Spanish sounding name, Calle Vista. Road with a view. On a hunch I turned up Calle Vista, and almost immediately the Chevy started a long slow climb up a winding road. I didn't know where I would wind up but my sense of direction told me that the hill I was climbing would be somewhere south of Tara.

I navigated the sharp hairpin curves with ease, riding the centerline. There was no traffic and I could see far enough around the curves to get back on my side if a car approached toward me.

After a few minutes the road straightened out for a quarter of a mile or so and I saw a spot where I could get off on the shoulder, and slowed the Chevy.

The spot was a turnaround place, or a place for slower traffic to get off of the road. Cactus plants grew on the side of the hill that sloped steeply on my right. On my left, the hill rose another 300 feet or more with an occasional house here and there.

I looked to my right across the canyon. There below me was Tara in all of its 35-acre glory. I could see the house and the barn like they were toys in an Old MacDonald farm game. The two swimming pools reflected the morning sun brilliantly.

I dug out a pair of high-powered binoculars, scooted to the passenger side of the Chevy, rolled down the window and took a look at the ranch below me.

Behind the barn I caught sight of several men in light blue denim uniforms moving what first appeared to be bales of hay. I turned the focus knob on the binoculars and zoomed in closer.

Expensive hay. The bundles were very much like the ones stacked up row after row in the pictures next to Thad Yates.

Apparently they were just finishing up their task. Two of the men hoisted the last of the bales into the back of a moving van and lowered the door. One of the men waved at someone in the van, and the van started to move. The other man turned and walked to a beat-up green and white Ford pickup truck and got in. I couldn't see the man behind the wheel of the truck until the truck pulled away and did a U turn in the driveway behind the barn.

When it headed back towards the paved road that encircled Tara, I could see the driver clearly.

It was my friend Ernesto.

The van was already on the blacktop by the time Ernesto and his passenger arrived in the Ford. I watched the left turn signal blink off and on and the van turned left, followed the road around the ranch and to the main gate. The truck was thirty yards behind.

The van stopped at the main gate and waited a few minutes for the gate to open, then went through. The Ford pickup accelerated enough to get through the gate behind the van and they both turned left, back towards Soledad Canyon Road.

I hit the zoom button again on the binoculars and brought the Ford into clear, close-up view. I could read the license plates on the truck. I popped open the glove box, grabbed a pen and wrote the license number on the back of my hand.

I got the Chevy started and I whipped around and headed down the hill much faster than I had climbed it. Hoping I could catch sight of the van or the truck before they reached the freeway, I sped down the hill as fast as I could navigate the curves without running the risk of meeting another car head-on.

By the time I reached the corner of Calle Vista and the blacktop leading to Soledad Canyon Road, I could tell that I was not going to be able to determine which way the van and pickup had turned. I glanced left towards the entrance to Tara. They were out of sight.

I stomped on the gas and silently cursed my ancient, trusty Chevy for not having any guts. The engine coughed, then gradually picked up RPMs and I was doing sixty by the time I passed the gate at Tara and whipped out onto Soledad Canyon. Fortunately there is no traffic on Saturday mornings.

When I got to the Lancaster Freeway on-ramp, I mentally flipped a coin, heads equals southbound, and tails equals northbound. I chose tails and whipped the wheel hard right just in time to catch the northbound on-ramp.

The little Chevy purred up the ramp and I hit the freeway at 70 miles per hour, swung over two lanes and goosed the old car again. The speedometer crept up slowly to 80 then 90 and peaked out at 97 miles per hour.

I passed two cars, neither of which were of interest. By this time I was reaching the peak of a hill which crested out above Palmdale valley. I could see for four miles down the freeway, straight as an arrow. There wasn't another vehicle in sight.

Oh, well, wrong choice, I thought.

I took the Antelope Valley freeway exit, got off at the first spot and swung under the Lancaster Freeway, then right on the on-ramp to the southbound side. I knew I could never catch up with the truck and van on the southbound freeway, but I had to go that way to get back to my place in Long

Beach anyway, so I relaxed and drove at the speed limit.

By the time I got back to the apartment it was nearly five o'clock and I was more hungry now than mad, so I parked the Chevy, went in and began digging through the cupboards and refrigerator trying to find something to eat.

I am not a big eater. I get hungry and I eat, then I may not get hungry again for ten or twelve hours. But I always try to eat something when I first feel that twinge of hunger. Maybe that is why I have been able to keep my weight at about 175 pounds when most men after they turn 30 start to put on a spare tire.

I don't exercise a whole lot. Twice a week I attend Karate classes, hoping to someday get a black belt. But other than that I don't run or play tennis, and I eat pretty much what I want. If I have it on hand.

If not, I know a hundred restaurants around the South Bay area where I can get whatever it is I am hungry for. Tonight I wanted Mexican food.

I got undressed, showered, shaved and put on a nice pair of blue slacks and a light blue pullover shirt. I chose a pair of white Nike shoes and glanced at myself in the mirror as I picked up my bedroom phone and dialed Pat Collete's number.

I was hoping I could catch her at home and make arrangements to meet her after her show at the Cloister. She didn't answer but her machine did. I left a message that I would try to stop by around midnight.

I left the apartment and headed the Chevy south. A long legged lady in a tight swimming suit was on my mind.

CHAPTER 18

The door opened slowly after I knocked. She stood there a second like she didn't recognize me, then slowly a smile appeared on her face.

"Bob!" she said.

"Yep, it's me, dry clothes and all," I said.

"What a pleasant surprise," she giggled. "Come in."

"Actually, I came by to see if you would like to join me for dinner. I'm hungry for Mexican food, and I'm headed for El Torrito's"

"That is amazing!" she said.

"It is?" I asked. "What's so amazing about being hungry for Mexican food?"

"My friend and I were just leaving to go to dinner, and he mentioned Mexican food."

"Your friend?" I asked, a cold feeling sweeping over me.

The door opened a little wider and I could see her friend standing behind her. He put a huge arm around her waist and smiled at me.

"Hi!" he said, friendly enough.

My heart sank in my chest. I should have called first, but my racing imagination told me that I would find her at home, anxiously waiting for me to drop by and ask her out for dinner.

And after dinner she would ask me in for a drink. And after the drink we would go swimming in the pool with no clothes on.

"Oh," I muttered.

"Bob, this is Ronnie," she said, sliding aside so that I could meet her friend. He stuck out a huge hand.

"Ronnie Duncan, sir," he said.

I shook hands, hoping he wouldn't crush my small one.

"Hello," I said, with as much enthusiasm as I could muster.

"Ronnie and I have known each other for years," she said. "We kind of grew up together."

"Oh," I said again.

"Won't you join us, Bob?" he asked.

"Well, I, uh, that is I, guess I should be going..."

"Please, Bob," she said, "We can have Mexican food, if that is what you wanted."

It wasn't EXACTLY what I wanted, but now wasn't the time to go into that, so I meekly agreed to join them for dinner.

We took Ron's car. I sat in the back seat, feeling like a high school tag-a-long without a date.

El Torrito's is a chain of Mexican restaurants in southern California known for its atmosphere and fine Sonora style Mexican food. All of their restaurants are built with the same basic theme, like a hacienda, four outside walls with a patio or courtyard in the middle. The outside walls have booths, the courtyard tables.

They usually have a waiting period of fifteen or twenty minutes before you can get a table. We waited at the bar.

Sipping Margaritas and making small talk, I found out that Ron taught Rhonda karate at a school owned by a nationally known chain. I remembered how fast Hair had moved at the barn at Tara, and thought that big men CAN move fast. Ron was probably a good example.

We talked karate styles for a while, and I mentioned meeting a guy recently who was as big as an elephant but fast as a cat.

"Sounds like someone I know." Ron said.

"You probably don't know this guy," I said, "He's a pretty shady character."

"What does he look like?" Ron asked.

"Well, he's about six-two weighs about 250 and has hair all over his ugly body," I said.

"That must be Hair," Ron said.

I almost choked on my margarita.

"You do know him!"

"He trained with me for about five years," he said, "That was back a few years ago when Hoss MacMillan trained with me."

"You trained Hoss?" I gulped.

"Yeah, he was one of my first students when I opened my first dojo. That was back before I joined the national chain."

My mind raced. I had lied to Rhonda about who I was and why I was in her yard. Now I needed to find out more about Hair, but why would a meter reader be interested in two guys who were well known thugs?

I decided it was time to confess.

"Can I trust you two with a story?" I started.

"Well, if it's about Hoss or Hair, it's probably common knowledge," Rhonda said.

"Actually, it's about me," I said. "My name isn't Bob and I am not a meter reader."

"You're not?" Rhonda glanced at me in surprise, then at Ron.

I looked at Ron and something told me that here was a guy that didn't care what someone did for a living. If he liked you he was going to be a friend, unless of course you crossed him. In that case, I thought, he could be a deadly enemy.

I decided to trust them.

"My name is actually Kip Yardley," I said, sheepishly.

"And just what WERE you doing in my yard, Mr. Yardley?" Rhonda asked icily.

"Well, I am a private detective," I said.

"What makes you think I'm going to swallow that one?" she asked, glancing at Ron again. "First you're a meter reader, now you're a private detective?"

"I know you have every reason to be angry," I said. "I was in your yard because I had been over the rear wall and into the house behind you. Steve Lang's house."

"Why didn't you just go in his front door?" Ron asked.

"The Long Beach police have a guard in the yard," I said.

"Did you know Steve?" Ron asked.

"No. I was retained by his sister, Starla, to find his killers. She believes that the police are not going to investigate his death sufficiently to find out who killed him."

"I believe you," Ron said.

Rhonda turned to me and grinned.

"Well, if he believes you, so do I!" she said.

"I'm telling you the truth," I said. "I searched Steve Lang's house to try to find a clue to his death. Police had it taped off and they get funny about private detectives searching where they have already searched."

"Did you find anything you could use?" Ron asked.

I hesitated to say anything. I liked this guy, but I wasn't sure which way he would go. He had known Hoss MacMillan and he knew Hair, and that may or may not make him an enemy.

"Before I answer that, what do you think of this Hairy guy?"

"Hair?" he laughed. "I think he's got himself into something that he will regret. I haven't seen him in over a year, but I heard he married Hoss's widow, or Hoss's ex wife, to be more exact."

Again I almost swallowed my Margarita. This time while it was still in the glass.

"Hair married Hoss's ex?" I gasped.

"You didn't know that?" he asked.

"What kind of private detective are you if you didn't know that?" Rhonda asked.

"That's a good question, Rhonda," I said. "I guess I just haven't had the time to track down those facts. I knew that she had remarried, to a biker type, but I didn't connect that with Hair."

"Ron and I don't mean to poke fun at your abilities," Rhonda smiled.

"No, that's O.K." I said. "You've given me some important information. I don't know what it means yet, but I have a feeling I am going to find out soon."

"What do you mean?" Rhonda asked.

"I intend to pay Mr. and Mrs. Hair a visit," I said.

We chatted a few minutes until our table was ready and moved to the dining room.

I ordered enchiladas and a Dos Equiis beer. As we ate, I explained to my new friends the circumstances under which I had met Hair. I told them about my investigation, feeling that I had met someone whom I could trust. They listened intently and when I was through, Ron spoke.

"I've known for a long time that Hoss was into drugs and that someday it would get him killed. He used to say that there wasn't anyone big enough or smart enough to kill him. He laughed when we told him that drug lords are not ordinary people. They don't get to be drug lords by being nice."

"Do you think he was killed by a rival drug gang?" I asked.

"I don't know," he said. "I think he probably stepped on a few toes in the underground. There's always someone bigger than you when you get involved in drug activity. My God, the Mafia is the big drug lord. No one in their right mine would cross them. If they can get a president, they can get anyone."

"You think the Mafia got Kennedy?" I asked.

"I do, with the aid of the CIA," Rhonda said, putting her fork down. "Have you seen the movie?"

I knew she was talking about a popular motion picture that depicted the investigation of the Kennedy assassination by a New Orleans district attorney. In the movie, the Mafia was the prime suspect in Kennedy's assassination, paid by the CIA.

"Yeah," I said. "I agree with you, but it's never going to be proven."

"You're right," Ron said. "The number one police force in the world will not go down."

"They can do anything they want under the heading of national security. Congressional inquiries can't touch them. The President can't touch them, the Senate can't touch them. They control the FBI and the Secret Service. They are just too powerful."

"They weren't supposed to be that powerful," Rhonda said. "During the cold war, they just started getting away with things and implicating people who are powerful, until now they are their own little empire. The director himself can't control them."

We finished our meal. I picked up the tab over Ron's objections and we left.

On our way back to Rhonda's I was surprised and glad to learn that Ron and Rhonda were just good friends. But there was little chance that Rhonda was going to spend the night with me with Ron around so I said good-bye at the curb, climbed into my Chevy and drove away thinking that it had been a productive evening.

CHAPTER 19

It was ten fifteen. I headed the Chevy north on the 605 Freeway, hoping that I could get to Hollywood and the Cloister nightclub in time to catch Pat's last show. Traffic was light and with any luck I should be able to make it in 45 minutes.

But luck is not my long suit. It started to sprinkle just enough to make me turn on my windshield wipers by the time I crossed the Santa Monica freeway. By the time I hit the interchange it was pouring.

It is true what the song says about California. It never rains in California. It pours.

My windshield wiper blades had deteriorated in the sun to the point where little slivers of rubber were hanging off of them. It was all I could do to see the white lines and keep in my lane. Traffic started to back up as I hit the Hollywood freeway and I decided to get off and call the club, leave a message for Pat that I would meet her at her place.

I found a Standard station open and a well lit phone booth. In some parts of LA you don't want to get out of your car, but this place was well lit and I had my pawn-shop special in my jacket pocket. A female answered the phone at the Cloister and I asked if Pat had started her last show. She had, so I left a message to have her meet me at her place.

Back in the Chevy, I figured I had time to kill so I headed north on Vermont and hit Sunset Boulevard, swung right and headed for Pat's place off Silverlake.

A mile from Dodger Stadium, I got bogged down in traffic again. The Dodgers opening day traffic, I thought. I turned on the radio to see if I could catch the final score, or to see if the game had been called because of rain.

Cars ahead of me stopped to let traffic from Elysian Parkway get on Sunset. I glanced at a car getting on. It was a red late model Camaro. Just as the Buick in front of me started to move, a pickup truck swung off Elysian Parkway and cut in front of the Buick.

It was a battered old Chevrolet pickup truck, green and white. I sat there waiting for the Buick to move and it suddenly sank in through the rain in my mind. The license plate wasn't visible on the truck, but I would bet twenty dollars that I knew what it was.

I glanced right to my side mirror. There was a space just vacant enough to squeeze into. I shot the Chevy to the right and pulled even with the Buick. A space opened in front of me, and the pickup truck cut into it.

The license plate was the same one I had seen on the pickup truck at Tara.

I stayed close behind the truck, when it changed lanes, I tried to change lanes too. Sometime I would have to wait a few cars, but as traffic got on the Five freeway northbound, Sunset cleared enough that I could pace the truck.

I dropped back four car lengths. I didn't want to spook the driver, if he recognized my car.

The truck exited Sunset, took a side street south a few blocks then turned east again. I didn't know the area very well, but I knew we were in East Los Angeles. The Barrio.

I was able to shadow the truck without difficulty. We finally got to a street I recognized, and just as I thought I knew where I was, the truck turned on Brooklyn and headed towards Fourth Street. There is a string of Mexican bars between Fourth and First streets on Brooklyn.

Even with the windows rolled up I could hear the pounding bass of the Mexican rock bands radiating from the bars.

The truck slowed. I dropped back another car length. I watched the tail lights on the truck come on. It stopped next to a Datsun near the corner of Second Street, then backed into a parking place.

I drove by and glanced at the joint.

La Caribbean.

The next open parking place was a block away near First. I parked, locked the Chevy, and walked back up Brooklyn, the heavy 9mm pistol swinging in my jacket pocket.

CHAPTER 20

The noise in La Caribbean was so deafening I almost didn't go in. I can't stand loud music; it drives through my skull like a bulldozer. One of the reasons my ex-wife and I split up is because she was 17 when I married her. I was 25. By the time I was 35, she was only 27, and still liked to party.

She loved the rock and roll scene. I couldn't stand it.

Inside the club I tried to blank my mind to the music and the noise. I glanced around and noticed that the place was nearly empty. To my right was the bar; it ran front and back of the place. To my left was a row of booths. Ahead of me was a bathroom area and a rear exit.

The place was laid out very similar to the Zanzabuku. I made my way to the bar and in my best Spanish, ordered a beer.

No one even glanced at me. I paid for my beer, took a sip and slowly let my eyes take in the customers.

The place was not very well lit. Smoke hung like steam from a cauldron over the bar. The bartender was in his sixties, balding and wrinkled.

Behind me, at the second booth sat three men, jabbering away excitedly in Spanish.

I listened as well as I could. Between the noise and my limited knowledge of Spanish, I could barely make out what they were jabbering about. The subject was marijuana.

I watched the bar mirror to see if I could make out any of the faces.

Just then one of the men slid out of the booth and headed for the rest rooms in the rear. It was Ernesto.

I let him get in the men's room, then took a long drink of beer and headed in after him.

He didn't look around when I went in.

I put the barrel of the gun an inch below his skull and pulled the hammer back.

"Shake the dew off your melon, Ernesto. Let's walk."

"O.K., man, take it easy, man," he said.

I opened the door and looked towards the booth. The two men were arguing, gesturing back and forth. The bartender was watching the bandstand where a trumpet player blared the high notes of a Mexican song.

I shoved Ernesto out in front of me, took his shoulder and turned him towards the rear exit.

Outside, he stopped.

"Keep moving, senor!" I ordered.

He moved again. I motioned towards the front of the building.

We turned the corner and headed down Second Street. At Brooklyn I nudged him left and walked him towards my car.

"We're going for a little ride, Ernesto," I said.

"Whatever you say, man, you're the man," he said.

"You'd better damned well believe it," I said.

We reached the Chevy and I motioned him to get in the driver's seat.

I walked around the front of the car, the gun at my waist and concealed from casual passersby.

I handed him the keys and told him that I didn't mind getting blood all over the inside of my car if he tried to get cute.

"Where we go, man?" he asked.

"Shut up, and just drive like I tell you," I said.

I had him turn on First Street and go south to Soto. After a few more turns, I had him pull the car into the parking lot at the pawnshop where I had bought the gun.

"Let me tell you something, Ernesto," I said. "You are going to answer some questions for me, and if you don't tell me the truth I will blow that greasy head of yours all over the parking lot. Then I'll wipe the prints off this gun and put it in your dead hand."

"I bought this gun right here in this pawn shop. It isn't registered to me. By all legal means it belongs to the pawn shop".

"If you should die here, with a gun in your hand that belongs to this pawnshop, the cops will think you took the gun and blew your own brains out. Comprende?"

I didn't have the foggiest idea what I was talking about, but I hoped that he would take the bluff.

"Si!"

"O.K. Now first, who shot Gary with my gun and tossed his corpse in the hole under the barn?"

"Hair shot him, Senor."

He looked at me pleadingly. I guessed my bluff was working.

"Where is my gun?" I asked.

"One of the men I was with has it," he said. "I sold it to him."

"Which one of the men?" I asked.

"The little one, Senor."

"Second question, who was Hair referring to when he said that the boss might not want me dead?"

"I do not know, Senor."

I cocked the hammer back on the automatic.

"Honest, Senor, I don't know who gives the orders. I just do what Hair tells me," he whined.

"Where were you moving the marijuana to?"

"We moved it to the back of a topless bar in Hawthorne," he said.

"What's the name of the bar?"

"I think it is called the Bucket," he said.

"Did you sell it to someone at the Bucket?" I asked.

"I don't know, Senor, I just delivered it there. I didn't take any money."

"One more question," I said. I was fishing now, but I thought I might as well play my hand out, "Who killed Steve Lang?"

"I don't know, Senor. I don't even know Steve Lang is dead."

"Do you know who Steve Lang is? Or was?"

"No, Senor. I didn't know this guy."

For some strange reason I believed him. By now he probably knew that I wasn't going to shoot him, but I still had a score to settle.

"Get out of the car and put your hands on the hood, Ernesto."

He did as he was told. I got out at the same time on the passenger side and walked around the front. The motor was still running.

I stopped two feet away from him and uncocked the hammer, slid the Colt into my pocket.

"O.K. Ernesto," I said, "Now we face each other like men. Is this what you wanted? You still think you can take me, make your move."

"Oh, I don't want any trouble, Senor." he said.

"Maybe you don't, but I do," I said.

"Senor, don't, I don't want to fight with you, I was just following orders. Hair would kill me if I didn't follow his orders."

"Shut up, Ernesto. Take your best swing."

He looked at me. The look in his eyes betrayed his meek attitude. I knew he would stick a knife in me if he had a chance.

I reached in the inside pocket of my jacket and got a switchblade knife with a five inch blade. I showed it to him, flipped the switch and watched his eyes as the blade sprang into view. He didn't flinch.

I dropped the knife at his feet.

"There's your big chance, Ernesto," I said. "Go for it."

He looked at me with hatred in his eyes, glanced at the knife, and back at me.

"I won't do this, Senor," he said.

Frustrated, I faked a punch at his face and when he moved his hands to block, I swept him off his feet with my left foot. He fell backwards. I stepped back and waited. He looked at the knife.

When he picked it up, I waited again. He got up on one knee holding the knife out in front of him. I waited.

When he was on his feet, I turned my back on him and took a step. I knew when he lunged. I dropped to my left hand, whirled and kicked.

The kick caught him in his right knee and I heard it snap. I sprang to my feet, whirled and lashed out with both fists simultaneously, one high, one low. Both landed. One snapped his nose, the other cracked a rib at his solar plexus.

He grunted, but refused to go down. I faked a kick at his midsection, leaped and kicked him in the throat with a right roundhouse kick. This time he went down.

I retrieved my knife, got in the Chevy and left Ernesto with both hands at his throat, spitting blood.

CHAPTER 21

It didn't take but two minutes to get back to La Caribbean. The little guy was still sitting at the table where he had been. The other man was gone, presumably to look for his friend, Ernesto.

I sat across the table at the booth. The little man looked at me as I sat down. His glazed eyes told me that he had either had too many beers or smoked too many joints.

"Give me the gun, cabron," I said.

"Who are you, man?" he asked.

"Never mind that. Listen for a minute."

The band was on break, the jukebox wasn't playing, and you could hear a pin drop in the bar. I had the Colt under the table. I snapped the hammer back hard.

His eyes started to get wider, and for a second the glaze seemed almost to disappear.

"O.K. man," he said. "Whatever you say, man."

"Just put it on the table, cabron," I said.

I watched his eyes as he brought his hands to his chest, then slowly slid his right hand under his jacket.

"Use two fingers, and think about what you're doing," I said. "If you get funny I will shoot your balls off."

"No, man, I'm just gonna do what you say, man." His eyes were watering, and his voice had started to quaver.

I glanced around. The place was nearly empty and the balding bartender was watching a Mexican show on the television.

The gun hit the table with a slight "chunk" and he pulled his hand back like the gun handle had been hot. I picked up the gun and stuck it in my jacket pocket.

"If you even think about squealing when I walk out of here, I'll come back and blow your skinny little ass to Tijuana," I said.

I got up and left. I didn't hear a sound behind me.

Outside, I got in the Chevy, started the motor and drove back towards the interchange.

My entire trip to East Los Angeles had taken well over an hour. I glanced at the digital clock on the dash, saw that it was almost two.

Pat would be home by now, but probably mad as hell because I wasn't there.

I found the Chevron station that I had called the club from and used the phone again. She answered on the first ring.

"Kip, where are you?"

"I got tied up," I said. "I wanted to let you know how sorry I am for standing you up like this."

"I'm used to it," she said, sighing. I knew that she was lying; no woman ever gets used to being stood up. They eventually just get over it. At the same time, they get over the guy who stands them up.

"Pat, forgive me. I ran into an old enemy, and I had to take a few minutes to let him know that pay backs are hell."

"Yes, darling, they are," she said. I thought I detected a note of sadness in her voice.

"I'll make it up to you," I said. "I promise I'll come over whenever you want me to. You name the day."

"How about the sixth Sunday of next month?" she said, and hung up.

CHAPTER 22

The next morning, Sunday, I woke up with an idea. I had sat up late after getting back to my apartment from La Caribbean and my disappointing phone call to Pat. She had a right to be mad at me, and I was feeling a little melancholy when I got home, so I sat up till four watching old movies on television and drinking beer.

I knew from days past that Pat never worked on Sundays. My idea was just to drop in on her. No phone calls, just show up at her door.

It was nearly eleven when I woke up. I got out of bed and rushed through a shave and shower. By the time I cooked a bowl of oatmeal my stomach was reminding me that I had stayed up too late, drank too much beer and was pushing myself too hard lately.

I dumped the oatmeal in the sink, ran some water on it and flipped on the garbage disposal. So much for breakfast.

The air smelled clean as I left the apartment and headed the Chevy north on the freeway. It always smells clean and good after a heavy rain. Once I had entertained the idea of inventing a smog control device that would run the exhaust through a series of spray baths to take the impurities out of it before dumping it out the tail pipe.

In college I had written some scathing articles about the smog problems around the South Bay area.

Things had improved since I went to college; the air had cleaned up considerably, but it was still bad.

This morning, though, it was good. I breathed deeply with the window down on the driver's side of the Chevy.

There was hardly any traffic on the freeway. I made it to Pat's place in Hollywood in forty minutes.

I rang the bell twice and waited. No answer. I jiggled the button again and waited. Still no answer.

Concerned, I used a key she had given me early in our relationship, and let myself in.

Pat wasn't at home.

Her apartment had been ransacked. Someone had done a real good job of searching for something. Drawers were pulled out and dumped either on the floor or on her bed. All of the places I would have looked for something had been tried. This didn't look like a police search, it looked like a pro job. Now I was really concerned.

There was no sign of violence. Nothing was broken, no overturned furniture or tables. No lamps knocked off tables.

The place had just been combed thoroughly for something. But what? And more importantly, by whom?

I called Toby. He listened intently while I detailed the state of the apartment, then advised me to call the LA police. He gave me the name of a detective sergeant Tillotson that he knew, who worked burglaries.

I called Tillotson. My concern was Pat's whereabouts. He asked me if I knew of any relatives, and I told him that she had a family back in Chicago, but no relatives that I knew of in Southern California.

He wanted to know about friends. I told him what I knew. Pat had a few friends that she knew from being in show business. Some aspiring actors, some film crews.

He advised me to wait for him at Pat's, but I had other plans. I would start my own search for Pat. Let him handle the break-in.

I hung up and started calling around.

A friend from the Cloister told me Pat had mentioned to her that her agent was working on a deal with a top Las Vegas hotel to book her for three months, six shows a week. She said that Pat might have gone to Las Vegas with her agent. Funny she didn't mention it to me, I thought.

I hung up and dialed the hotel in Las Vegas. I got the registration desk and asked if Pat Collette was registered there. The answer was no. I asked if she had reservations there and got another no.

I sat at Pat's kitchen table and thought about things. I needed to pay a visit to Hair and Mrs. Hair, the former Mrs. Hoss MacMillan. Problem was I didn't know where to start looking for them. If it wasn't Sunday I would go to city hall and find the marriage license, get an address, and be on my way. Never on Sunday.

I decided to ask some questions at the Bucket in Hawthorne. If Ernesto had been straight with me, and I believed he had been, there might be someone at the Bucket that could give me some answers.

It's a long drive from Hollywood to Hawthorne even on Sundays. I took the San Diego freeway south and got caught up in Airport traffic around Century, but soon made it to El Segundo Boulevard and exited. A short drive east and a left turn put me on Hawthorne Boulevard.

The Bucket at one time was just a quiet neighborhood bar, where friends played shuffleboard and pool at a small eight ball table. In the seventies a string of topless and nude bars started springing up around the airport. The owner of the Bucket refused to run his bar as a nudie joint, and refused to sell.

They found him hanging from a tree in his backyard, an apparent suicide. Most of the cops I knew thought otherwise, but there were no leads and the coroner eventually ruled suicide.

I knew his daughter. She was the girlfriend of a friend of mine from college days. She told police that a big man with short blond hair had visited her father. The description fit Hoss MacMillan.

Shortly afterward, Hoss opened the Bucket in the same spot where the old bar had been. He had it remodeled with several booths on both sides, a horseshoe shaped dancing stage projecting out into the room, barstools around the edge of the stage.

As I entered a tall brunette with very shapely breasts was dancing seductively to the beat of a song. The words kept repeating themselves "it's not your imagination...it's not your imagination."

I found a spot away from the stage and ordered a beer from another very shapely girl who wore the bottom of a bikini and a tee shirt on top. The tee shirt was not very concealing.

I drank my beer and looked around the place, trying to judge which room the marijuana would be stashed in. When I caught the waitress's eye, I ordered another beer and asked if there was a large unused room in the back.

"Not to my knowledge," she said. "We use the room behind the stage for a dressing area before we go on."

"Is there a basement?"

"Yeah, there's part of one. It doesn't go under the front of the building, just the back."

I tipped her generously and sipped my beer, wondering what my next move should be.

I left part of my beer on the table and walked to the back of the place, ostensibly looking for the restroom. I found the men's room and glanced around before I went in.

There was a door with an EXIT sign over it down the hall to my right. In front of me was the men's room. Behind me was the room that was used as a dressing room by the dancers.

I eased back to the door under the EXIT sign, and tried the knob. It turned, and I opened the door and stepped out into the alley behind the bar. There was no knob on the outside of the door so I stuck a book of matches between the latch and the frame so that the latch wouldn't engage.

The area I was in was the full width of the building, and ran ten feet or so to a high concrete block wall.

I walked the width of the building looking for a window indicating a basement. Nothing.

Against the wall was a dumpster, and beyond the dumpster was a steel double door which, when opened, would let the trash trucks pick up the dumpster.

I let myself back in, pocketed the book of matches and returned to a half empty beer at my table.

The brunette had finished her dance and was serving drinks; the blond who had told me about the basement was now starting her routine. I hesitated to ask any more questions. If the two girls put two and two together, they might wonder why I wanted to know about spare rooms.

Like most topless bars, the girls were required to serve drinks between dancing their routines. I decided to watch the show, drink my beer and ask Blondie a few more questions. She seemed willing enough to talk, particularly after the tip I gave her.

Three beers later, she finished her routine and came back on the floor to serve drinks. I asked her again about the basement.

"You sure are curious about basements," she said.

"Well I am from the County Health department," I lied.

"Oh!"

"I am supposed to make sure that if there is a basement in a building the business doesn't install toilets in it without permits."

"What kind of permit?" she asked.

"It's a sewer permit," I winged it. "You see, toilets in basements must have special type of flushing units, otherwise they might fill up from the sewer level being higher than they are."

She looked at me with all the innocence of an eight year old.

"I've never been down there," she said. "I don't think there is a toilet down there, though."

"How do you get to the basement?" I asked.

"The stairs are in the dressing room," she said.

I got up and started for the dressing room.

"You can't go in there," she said. "Jeannie might be undressed."

"I just watched Jeannie take every stitch of clothes off except her gold high heels," I said.

"I know, but it's different back there. You aren't supposed to see us nude until we want you to see us nude."

"Lady, I have a job to do," I said, hoping she wouldn't ask for credentials.

"Well you can just wait until I do my routine again, and I'll let you in the dressing room!" she said.

I sat down reluctantly and asked her for another beer. I was getting a little light headed, but if I had to wait I had better drink. The bouncers watch for guys that sip one beer and watch the girls dance for two hours.

She brought me the beer and I tipped her heavily again. She bent over close to me, the tee shirt fell away from her chest. I was suddenly very aware of the size of her breasts. She nibbled my ear and kissed me on the cheek.

"I wish I had a job like yours," she said. "I'm tired of dancing for a living. If it wasn't for nice guys like you, I'd quit this place."

I didn't reply. I was thinking that every guy who tips her is a nice guy, and she probably tells all of them the same thing.

By the time she went backstage I could feel my tongue getting fuzzy in my mouth. I always know when I have had enough beer. My tongue feels like it weighs thirty pounds and I get a greasy taste in my mouth.

I followed her to the door and she let me in the dressing room with her.

With the door closed, she turned and looked at me.

"Now you promise not to peek at me," she said.

"I promise," I said.

She started to take the tee shirt off and I started looking for the stairs to the basement. They were behind a low wall, the wall covered with a black velvet curtain. I started down the stairs.

"Well aren't you going to look?" she asked.

"You made me promise not to peek." I said.

"Oh, you!" she said. "Most men would peek anyway!"

I peeked.

She had removed the tee shirt and bikini bottom and replaced them with a red cowgirl outfit. The skirt was about three sixteenths of an inch lower than the lowest portion of the exact middle of her anatomy.

The top was a vest. The two halves of the vest covered only half of each breast. Her long blond hair had been pulled forward over her shoulders to cover the other halves of her breasts.

"Nice," I said.

"Thanks," she replied. "I get off at six."

I walked down the stairs. At the bottom of the dim stairwell I found a steel door with a hasp and a master padlock. A locksmith had taught me a trick years ago. If you take a master key and file all but the first notch down flush, about an eighth of an inch from the groove, it will open most padlocks. I had one on my key chain.

The lock opened effortlessly.

I swung the door open quietly and stepped inside. There was a light switch on the wall to my left, and I clicked it on. A four-foot fluorescent fixture with two bulbs in it flickered a few times and came to life.

The room was about sixteen feet wide and ran the width of the building. In the center of the room were the bales I had seen removed from TARA.

I counted them. There were twelve bales, stacked two high and six long. I picked up a top bale and judged its weight. It probably would weigh fifty to sixty pounds.

The bales were wrapped tight in burlap. The unmistakable odor of marijuana permeated the small room. On the second bale from my left, bottom row, I saw the initials SLDW.

I opened the door, stepped back into the stairwell and closed the door. I put the small padlock back on the hasp and locked it and went back up the stairs. At the top, I stopped and peered out. No one was about, so I exited through the door and returned to the table in the front of the club.

I waved down the brunette, gave her my card and asked her to give it to Blondie.

"You mean Lisa?" she asked.

"Yes, if that's her name." I said.

"Would you like another beer?" she asked.

"No thanks," I said, "I think I've had enough."

I waited for Lisa to finish her number and when she went backstage to change for her next number I left the club.

CHAPTER 23

Monday morning. I was at the hall of records when it opened at 9. It didn't take me long to find what I was looking for. A marriage license issued to Clarence Stoverly and Vanessa MacMillan. Mr. and Mrs. Hair. I wondered what Vanessa MacMillan looked like. She probably was so ugly that if you looked up the word "grotesque" in the dictionary you would see her picture.

The address given for Clarence Stoverly was in Inglewood, not far from The Bucket I had visited in Hawthorne.

Inglewood was once a thriving community of upper middle class. As the affluent blacks moved south out of the inner city, the upper middle class whites moved further south to Palos Verdes or Hollywood Riviera.

Most of the neighborhoods were well kept, but the influence of drugs had turned the downtown area into ghost town. Stores were for rent, some boarded up, most with broken windows and signs of abandonment.

Inglewood Avenue runs north and south and the address I was looking for was a small ranch house slightly south of Century Blvd.

The constant whine of jet aircraft engines will remind you that you are directly below the flight path for LA International Airport.

I found the house without difficulty and rang the doorbell.

I didn't know what to expect, so I had my hand on the butt of my Colt 9mm and wasn't at all prepared for the person who came to the door.

She was in her mid thirties, a lithesome five-three, pretty and curvaceous. Her long black hair hung loosely down to her waist. I was ready to apologize for getting the wrong address when she opened the door.

"Hello," she said.

"Good morning, Ma'am," I smiled my best smile. "I'm looking for someone that I thought might live here, but I guess I've got the wrong address."

"Well, who is it you're looking for?" she asked.

"I believe his name is Clarence Stoverly," I said. "But his friends call him Hair."

"You have the right address," she smiled.

"Is Clarence here?"

"No, but I am Mrs. Stoverly," she said. "May I help you?"

You could have knocked me down with a wet noodle. I remembered the comment Hair had made about pretty boys getting all the pretty girls, and I couldn't believe someone as pretty as this woman was married to the guy I knew as Hair.

My surprise must have shown.

"Is something wrong?" she asked.

"No, I just wasn't sure I had the right address," I said.

"Won't you come in, Mister....?"

"Smith," I said, hurriedly. "Paul Smith, I'm interested in purchasing a home in the neighborhood, and my real estate agent told me that Clarence had recently purchased this house, and that he wouldn't mind if I looked around to get a price comparison."

She stepped aside and held the door open. I hesitated, but then figured what the hay, and walked in.

"Your agent must be mistaken," she said. "My parents have owned this house since I was thirteen. That's been a long time."

"At least ten years," I said, smiling.

"You are very flattering," she said. "More like twenty years."

"NO!" I said.

"I'm past thirty three," she said. "Until my former husband and I got married, I was a professional dancer."

"You don't say!" I said.

"Well, I was," she said. "I have made as much as five hundred dollars for eight hours of dancing."

Her smile faded. She glanced at me and a sad looked crossed her face.

"I was married to Hoss MacMillan," she said.

"I'm sorry, I don't recognize that name," I lied.

"He owned a string of topless and nude bars. We divorced a while back. He didn't treat me very well. Fortunately he didn't take me out of his will, and now I own the bars. I might even go back to dancing in them."

"Oh," I muttered.

"He's dead now; he was shot down two weeks ago."

"Oh," I muttered.

"The police still don't have any idea who killed him, but I have a sneaky feeling that I know."

"Oh!" I yelled.

She jumped back, startled. I tried to hide my excitement.

"Bad back," I said. "An old football injury, when I move my neck a certain way it hurts."

She smiled.

"I think that he was killed because he refused to play along with a crooked scheme to get a certain politician elected to a certain office."

"What office would that be?" I asked, trying to show only mild curiosity.

"Would you like a drink, Mr. Smith?" she asked.

"Oh, no, I never drink unless I'm alone or with somebody," I said.

The play on words alluded her.

"Well, I would like to chat more with you Mr. Smith," she said, "But I have some things to do, so if you don't mind..."

"Oh, not at all," I lied. I did mind. I wanted to know more about her sneaky feelings.

"Perhaps I could call you when you are not busy and we could chat some more on the phone?" I said.

"Hair doesn't like for me to talk to guys on the phone," she said.

"What kind of work does Clarence do?" I asked.

"He's unemployed right now," she said. "He occasionally does some moving."

"Oh, a moving company," I said, "If you give me the name of the company, maybe I'll call them when I find a house that suits me."

"Oh he doesn't work for a moving company," she shook her head.

"He just does some moving for a politician here in town, and now that I own the bars, he kinda works for me."

"I see," I said, although I didn't.

"I really must get some things done, Mr. Smith," she said.

I got up, told her that she could give Clarence a message for me and she asked if I would like to write it down.

"No, just tell him 'what goes around. comes around,'" I said.

"Will he know what that means?" she asked.

"Probably not," I said. I thanked her and left.

In the Chevy, I got a notebook and made a few notes next to the scribbling I had collected.

Hair does some moving for a politician.

The politician has political ambition.

The politician may have been responsible for Hoss's death.

By the time I got back to my apartment, I was starting to formulate an idea. So far it was just a hunch, but things were starting to make sense a little at a time.

CHAPTER 24

I knew as soon as I opened my door that something was wrong, but before I could think about it something hit the back of my head with the combined energy of a Hank Aaron homer and a double vodka martini on an empty stomach.

The lights just went out suddenly.

When I came to the edge of consciousness the pain set in like moss on a swamp pond. I felt very sick to my stomach, and my head throbbed with an uncontrollable pain.

I knew that I needed more than just meditation to cure this one.

I crawled to the phone to dial for help. The phone line had been cut; all I got was silence.

Sometime after dark I climbed out of the black pit again into a semi-conscious level. The pain had subsided a little. That was like saying your girl friend was just a little bit pregnant.

I managed to get to my feet and staggered out the door of my apartment and banged on a neighbor's door.

Richard Reames is a quiet bachelor who lives next to me, and one whom I would never bother if it wasn't in an emergency. We spoke when we saw each other, had even attended a Dodger baseball game together once, but we're not real close.

He took one look at me and dialed 911. An ambulance hauled me to Long Beach Community Hospital and they took pictures of my skull, tested my reflexes and told me that I was a very lucky man. I had a slight concussion and what appeared to be a very slight crack at the base of my skull. They wanted to keep me overnight for observation, but when I told them that I had suffered a fractured skull in the service, and that the crack was probably just an old injury showing up on x-rays, they released me.

I called a cab and went home. The apartment had been ransacked, almost as carefully as Pat's. Whatever the guy had been looking for I don't think he found; if he had found it he would have been gone when I came back and interrupted his search.

I opened a can of pork and beans and threw some hot dogs in a pot, poured the beans on top of them and set them on the stove.

After eating, my stomach felt a little better and the pain had eased back to a mild roar in my head. I could even think a little.

The first thing that I attempted to think about was what in the hell was so important that someone would search Pat's apartment, then mine, and damned near kill me in the process.

I went to the refrigerator and looked in the freezer section. The frozen marijuana package was still there, so if that was what the searcher was looking for, he surely would have found it. As I sat at the kitchen table it suddenly dawned on me that it wasn't the marijuana that someone wanted.

It was the pictures of the marijuana!

I remembered that I had opened my notebook after leaving Stoverly's house, and had stuck the photos in the book. I had then shoved the book under the front seat of my car.

Still dizzy, shaking like a leaf, I left the apartment door open and half-walked, half-ran to my car in the carport. I jerked the door open and felt under the seat. The notebook was gone.

I looked up and noticed that the glove compartment door was down, papers and my box of phony badges were strewn across the seat. Someone had searched the car, found what they were looking for, and left everything else.

I was certain now that the pictures had a definite tie to this case. The problem that I faced was figuring out what that tie might be.

I returned to the apartment, opened a beer and sat down on the couch. I flicked on the television but couldn't get interested in the ball game. The Dodgers were in San Diego, and the Padres were winning, but the game meant nothing to me. I turned off the set and rewired the telephone.

I was deep in thought when the phone rang, momentarily frightening me.

"Hello," I muttered.

"Kip, Darling."

"Pat? Where are you?"

"I'm in Las Vegas. I was surprised to learn that you have been trying to reach me here. Is something wrong?"

"Has the LAPD talked to you?" I asked.

"No, Kip. Is something wrong?"

"No, nothing is wrong, Pat. I think I might have inadvertently got you involved in this case I've been working on, but I'm glad you decided to go to Vegas." I was genuinely glad that she had not been there when her apartment had been searched.

"What is it? Kip, I think it's time you told me what is going on."

"I went to see you Sunday morning. You were not at home, so I let myself in," I started.

"That's OK."

"That's not all," I said. "Someone had ransacked your apartment, looking for something that wasn't there."

"Ransacked? How? Why?"

"Well, I don't know how they got in. I called the LAPD, and I guess they investigated, but someone had searched your place looking for some photos that they eventually found. I just discovered a few moments ago that the photos were stolen from my car."

I purposely didn't tell her about my bump on the head.

"Kip, maybe you should back off and let the police handle this," she suggested.

"I think I have at least some of the answers, now, and I'm not going to give anything away to the police until I get some more facts. When I get what I want, they'll be the first ones I call."

"You'll call me, won't you, Kip?" she asked.

"Sure, honey," I said.

"Then I'll be home Monday night, Kip. Please call me."

I promised I'd call, and hung up.

I had an idea that the photos were important to someone who had overlooked an important fact. A newspaper photographer took those pictures. I had a feeling I knew where to find the negatives.

It was nearly midnight, but I couldn't wait for morning to find out if my hunch was right. I stuck my head under the cold water faucet in the kitchen sink and winced when the water stung the cut in my scalp. It had taken eight stitches to close the skin.

My head ached, and I felt like I could sleep for hours, but I knew from experience that sometimes things are important enough to do when you think about them. This was one of those times.

CHAPTER 25

It was cooler than it had been the last few nights. I suspected that rain was going to visit the coastline again shortly. I was thankful for the cool breeze kicking up salt spray along the beach as I parked the Chevy in Seal Beach.

The town was quiet; a local bar on the corner shed the only light on the sidewalk. I walked down Main Street, past the rows of shops and paused outside the door of the Surf Sound. There were no lights on in the office and the door was locked. I used a credit card to get in and it didn't take me long to find the darkroom.

I fumbled in the dark until I found the light switch, flipped on the overhead lights and closed the door behind me. There was the customary length of string hung across one side of the room, strings of negatives suspended from it. I removed each string, one at a time and held them up to the light. There were negatives of people smiling, holding something and shaking hands. There were football heroes stiff-arming their way into the end zone. There were cheerleaders stacked four high waving pompoms. There were a lot of pictures of a lot of things, but not the ones I was looking for.

I opened the door and flipped the light switch off and retreated back through the long hallway past the rest rooms until I found the desk with the nameplate DONNA MAE WILSON still on it. The desk drawers were locked but the edge of my pocketknife opened them. In the bottom right hand drawer of Donna's desk I found one of those little black plastic cases that 35-millimeter film comes in. I popped the lid off and looked inside.

A roll of negatives was coiled like a snake inside the container. I fished it out and walked back down the long hall to the darkroom. No need to attract attention by turning office lights on.

In the darkroom I again turned on the overhead light and closed the door. An automatic switch started a small fan blowing in the room, pulling in air from outside. I could feel moisture in the air.

I held the negatives up to the light. The first few shots on the roll were of people playing volleyball on the beach. Then there was three or four of an automobile accident, paramedics bending over a bloody little boy and a twisted bicycle.

Then I found the ones I expected to find. There was Thad Yates. There was one of several bundles of confiscated marijuana. There was Steve Lang pointing to the corner of one of the bales. I flipped on the viewer light on the table and laid the film flat. By adjusting the focus I could blow up the negatives.

The corner of the bale of marijuana that Steve Lang was pointing to had small letters in black....SLDW. Steve Lang...Donna Wilson.

CHAPTER 26

I rolled the negatives back up and stuck them in the plastic container and stuffed it in my pocket. When I turned the light switch off, the fan stopped and I opened the door.

I knew immediately that I was not alone in the building. There were no lights on. There were no sounds. There was a feeling.

I was thankful that I had turned off the lights in the darkroom before I opened the door. Now the person or persons in the building were just as unable to see me as I was to see them.

In practicing for a black belt in Karate, there is a kata that symbolizes finding yourself suddenly going from a lighted room to a totally dark room. In the first part of the kata your hands shade your eyes and gradually lets them get accustomed to the darkness. I did that part without thinking about it.

We had practiced bursting balloons in the dark. You entered a room, you had ten seconds to look around you and find a balloon. The lights then went out and you had to burst the balloon with a punch, a kick or a slap, in total darkness.

When you got good at that, another balloon was added and you had twenty seconds to study the room. After you were able to burst five balloons in this manner, you had passed another test for your black belt.

I had the feeling that my training was going to come in handy, and it did.

The first punch came from my right. I shifted and moved. The instinctive training took over and I sprang backwards in the narrow hallway. I could see only a very dim outline of my opponent.

The dark shadow moved quickly towards me, launching a front kick aimed at my mid-section. I sidestepped the kick, slid around it and let fly a backhand strike at the shadow's neck. I missed the neck and hit hard skull. My hand glanced upwards and I sprang back the other direction in the hall.

By now my eyes had accustomed themselves fully and I could make out that the shadow was tall, at least six feet, and thin. It moved again, towards me. This time I attacked.

I front kicked and connected with hard muscle tissue, not where I wanted the kick to land. The shadow had blocked with an upraised leg and I knew that I had kicked him on the thigh. That would make quite a bruise, but it wasn't enough to take him out.

He side-kicked towards my head and I ducked, spinning, launching a side kick of my own..low, aimed at the one leg that supported my opponent. This time I didn't miss. I felt the solid impact of a good kick and heard a snap.

The shadow dropped.

I could see a glinting object appear at the shadow's side and knew it was a gun. I found the doorknob to the darkroom and opened the door.

I sprang sideways into the darkroom as a deafening roar echoed through the hallway. A flash of light and the immediate stench of cordite filled my senses.

I jerked the 9MM out of my jacket pocket and fell to the floor, outstretched arms angled up. I heard the shuffle of feet on carpet and a moan as the shadow retreated towards the typesetting room.

I crawled on elbows and torso out into the hall. The shadow opened the door to the typesetting room and was briefly silhouetted as he went through the door.

I sprang to my feet and ran towards the door. I didn't want to be silhouetted when I went though the opening so I crouched as low as I could, swung the door open and dove into the typesetting room, arms outstretched, 9MM in my right hand.

I landed hard and rolled to my right quickly. Shots rang out. The whine of slugs hitting the concrete floor and ricocheting around the room told me that my opponent wasn't giving up without a fight.

I fired once at the flash from the other side of the room, and rolled again. A quick retort sent slugs screaming away from the concrete, inches from where my head had been.

I had an advantage. I had been in this room before, and although I wasn't studying five balloons, I had observed enough to know exactly where everything was. I knew that ahead of me and to my left was the linotype machine where the old man had sat clacking away.

I rolled to my left three times, got to my hands and knees, and crawled behind the ancient machine.

I remembered a single light bulb in a shaded, flexible shaft that the old man had used to illuminate his copy.

I found the shaft and let my hand slide up until I found the shade and the bulb. Silently I turned the bulb counter-clockwise until it came out of the socket.

I braced myself and stood up behind the machine, watching intently for any sign that might give me my opponent's position. I saw nothing but shadows. A filing cabinet, a long wooden table filled with boxes of type, and water cooler was on my right.

I drew back my hand and flung the light bulb as hard as I could in the direction of the filing cabinet. It exploded with a pop just seconds before my opponent's gun roared. I was ready this time and fired at the flash.

I heard him scream and heard the sound of metal hitting concrete.

I sprang to my right and dropped behind the wooden table. My opponent was hit, but was silent now. I knew from my previous visit that the light switch that controlled the overhead lights in this room was above my head.

I switched the gun to my left hand and snaked my right up the wall until I found the switch. I flipped on the lights.

The shadow was Twinkle Toes.

CHAPTER 27

He sat with his back against the back wall of the room, holding a bloody right forearm with his left hand. His gun lay three feet away on the floor.

I saw his eyes flick towards the gun and for a split second I thought he might try for it. He glanced back at me and smiled, pretty white teeth sparkling.

"Oh, it's you, Mr. Yardley," he said.

"Who did you expect, Peter Pan?" I asked.

"You are under arrest, Yardley," he said, sneering.

"For what? Shooting back at someone trying to shoot me? Besides, I've got the drop on you, not the other way around."

"If you know what's good for you, you will put your gun down and help me bandage this arm. It's a felony to shoot a law enforcement officer."

"You're a cop?" I asked.

"Los Angeles County Sheriff," he said. "I patrol this area, and I watched you break in to this place. I was trying to arrest you when you shot me."

"Nice try, Twinkle Toes," I said. "You followed me here after finding the photographs in my car. You're a smart guy. You knew that there must be negatives somewhere, so you waited for me to lead you to them."

He curled up his lip and looked at me.

"You'll never be able to prove that, Yardley."

"Maybe not, but I believe it's true," I said.

I could hear sirens in the distance and I knew I had to get out of this situation fast. If he was a cop it was a sure-fire bet that I would at least be detained, if not arrested.

"On your feet, Twinkle Toes," I said.

He put his good arm down and struggled to his feet.

There was a door with a sliding steel bar on the back wall. I figured it must lead to the rear of the building.

"Open that door," I said.

He slid the bolt with his good hand and turned the knob.

The door opened. I walked close to him, but not too close, and motioned him out. He exited the building, hobbling on one good knee, with me right behind him.

Once outside, I knew that a gun in my hand would mean instant suspicion by any observers, especially cops, so I dropped the gun in my jacket pocket, with my hand still grasping it, and nudged Twinkle Toes.

"Walk three paces ahead of me, and don't try to get cute," I said.

He started walking, slowly, on one good leg. We proceeded fifty yards or so down an alley and out onto the next street, between a pool hall and a liquor store.

"Turn right," I said.

He did as he was told and that was the last step he took.

CHAPTER 28

The top of his skull went flying away to his right. Blood splattered the wall inches from my head. Another shot sent stucco chips flying in my face.

I dropped to my knees and scrambled back into the alley.

We had passed a narrow opening getting to the street. I ran as hard as I could back to the opening and slid around the corner. It was as dark as pitch inside the narrow opening. I groped my way down the passage with my back against one wall, feeling for a door or a window.

I found a door and tried the knob.

With a great sigh of relief escaping my lips, the door opened. I stepped through and found myself in a passageway with the stench of beer and urine strong in the air. I could hear voices and then I heard the solid "crack" that the cue-ball makes when it hits its target. I was in the pool hall.

I walked casually towards the front, pretending to zip up my pants as I walked. I got a curious look from two guys at the eight-ball table, but they went back to their game.

A slightly built teenager wearing bright colored knee length shorts and a white tee-shirt started to approach me, saw the look on my face, and retreated behind a counter.

"Did you want to shoot some pool, sir?" he asked.

"Naw, I just had too much beer and had to drain some out," I said, grinning a fake, half-drunk grin.

"Thought I might try catching some sand sharks down under the pier," I added.

I walked to the front door and peered through the glass. I could see no one carrying a gun or running up the street.

"Looks like it might rain," I said, cheerily.

"The TV says it's going to," the boy said. "Better take your raingear if you're going to fish in this weather."

Something clicked in my head. Raingear.

I thought about another time, another place.

It was the garage of the Highway Patrol office in Santa Barbara where I had my first assignment. I was standing there looking out the door, watching the rain beat down on the paved parking lot.

"Did you get your raingear?" a voice was asking.

"No, I forgot the damned key," someone was saying.

"I'll be damned," the first voice said. "Well, I'll get the bolt cutters and we'll cut the lock off the gear locker again."

"Someone should replace that lock with a combination and then we wouldn't have to do this every time," a voice said in the memory cells of my mind.

Back in the present, I looked out the door of the pool hall. It had started to rain. I could see raindrops bouncing off the paved street in front. I saw the headlights of a car glancing in hundreds of directions off the falling rain. A red and blue light was flashing off and on. It was a patrol car.

I watched as the car passed, right to left, down the street, watched the tail lights blink off and on as it signaled a left turn at the next corner.

My mind flicked to the past channel.

"We would just forget the damned combination," a voice was saying.

"Naw, we'll make it something we can remember..like a license plate number or something," the voice that was speaking in my memory was whiny, high pitched, nasal.

Suddenly I knew what I didn't really want to know.

A lot of things started clicking, slowly at first and then speeding up like someone was gradually turning up the speed on a VCR while I was watching a movie.

I walked out into the rain and across the street into a parking lot. Red and white banners around the lot were snapping and popping in the wind. Rain beat down hard on my head, reminding me that I had recently been knocked senseless. Pain was etching its way into my consciousness like acid. I needed to rest. I needed to sleep. I needed to forget.

I realized that I was in a used car lot. The second door I tried to open was the front door of a big dark blue Lincoln Town Car. I got in and collapsed in the front seat, barely getting the door shut behind me.

CHAPTER 29

When I woke up I could sense the activity going on around me. I raised my aching head up far enough to look out of the back window of the car. It was still dark and hundreds of bright lights were shining around all over the place. People milled around in the street. Television crew trucks were parked next to the pool hall, huge banks of lights on top of them lit up the scene.

Police were all over the place. I saw a gurney covered with a white sheet being rolled towards an ambulance. No one accompanied the gurney, other than the attendant. That meant that the person under that sheet was dead.

At first I had trouble getting it all clear in my mind. Then I remembered the blur of red that had streaked across my vision when Twinkle Toes lost the top of his head. I raised my hand to my face and felt the crusted blood on my forehead. Thank God it wasn't my blood.

I realized that sooner or later someone might spot me in the big Lincoln, and that I would probably spend the rest of my life answering questions. They would find both my fingerprints and Twinkle Toe's in the print shop.

I used my knife to bypass the ignition switch on the Lincoln and the engine started with a purr. I pulled the gear shift lever down to drive and slowly, deliberately inched my way through the other cars to the street.

No one even looked my way when I pulled out into the street. I glanced in the rearview mirror and saw that the entire focus of attention was on the television crew.

Back on Pacific Coast Highway I made my way slowly to the San Diego Freeway, north to the 605 freeway and found my way back to my apartment. It was four-thirty in the morning when I let myself in and collapsed on the couch.

I slept until nine-thirty. When I woke up I realized that I was nearing the point where I would be hospitalized for sheer exhaustion if I didn't watch it. I got up and showered and dressed slowly, drank a pot of coffee and forced down a bowl of cereal.

I knew what I had to do. I just hated the thought of doing it.

I had parked the big Lincoln two blocks away from my apartment on a side street, knowing that the used-car lot owner would report it stolen. By now, I'm sure the cops would be looking for the car. I would be lucky if they weren't looking for me.

I figured it would take a day or two for them to match my prints from the print shop and connect me to Twinkle Toes. Maybe that would give me enough time to do what I didn't want to do.

I called a cab and had the driver take me to LA International Airport.

At the airport I rented a snazzy looking Olds Cutlass and headed for Inglewood. I had one more thing to check on and I hoped it would provide me with the remaining piece of the puzzle.

A short while later I was parked at the entrance to the alley that led behind the Bucket. I left the car, checked my pocket to make sure I had my gun, picked up my 35mm camera from the back seat and walked down the alley to the door behind the Bucket.

I glanced around, hoping I had missed a window to the basement during my previous visit. There were no windows, but I found an iron hatch cover. It had been there since the building was built, probably a chute for unloading trucks into the basement.

I examined the cover and went back to the car for the tire iron. By using it as a crow bar, I was able to crack the cast iron corners of the cover and soon had it off. I stooped and looked into the dark basement.

I couldn't see anything. I sat down in the alley and put my legs through the opening, then wriggled my hips and shoulders through, holding to the top of the frame where the cover had been.

I let myself drop and landed softly on my feet. A shaft of light came from the opening where I had just entered, but I could see nothing in the shadows. I made my way carefully to the foot of the stairs and found the light switch. I flipped on the switch and my heart sank.

The marijuana was gone.

CHAPTER 30

My plans suddenly seemed to vanish like the fog along Pacific Coast Highway when the sun finally breaks through. I thought I had it all figured out.

The way I saw it, someone wanted the negatives of the pictures bad enough to attempt to kill me. What I needed as protection were some more pictures of the marijuana.

I was certain that the initials SLDW were significant. I guessed that they meant Steve Lang and Donna Wilson. How it all tied together was the thing I wasn't certain about.

I was shooting in the dark.

I exited the building the same way I got in and made my way back to the rented car. I put the camera in the trunk and sat in the front seat with a pencil and a notebook, jotting down some ideas.

First, I felt that Hair was probably directly involved with killing at least three people, Steve Lang, Donna Wilson, and the beach bum that had been found in the barn at Tara.

Second, I reckoned that Hair was following orders. Just as Twinkle Toes had been following orders. The only problem here, I noted in the book, was that I wasn't sure who was giving the orders.

I hated to think that my friend Toby Smith was involved in this. But my recollection of the license plate with the word "raingear" seemed to point that way. He had set the combination to the raingear locker at the old Highway Patrol office to match the license plate number of his car. When I saw the license number, my mine registered the word "raingear" instead of the actual license plate number.

I put the notebook in the passenger seat and started the engine.

My plan had been to photograph the marijuana bales and then confront Toby with them. A lot of what I expected to happen after that depended on how Toby reacted.

Now I had nothing but a roll of negatives.

I headed the car for the South Bay Mall. I knew there was a one-hour photo lab there. I planned to have two sets of prints made and mail one of them to myself to my post office box, a little insurance package I had learned from watching television detectives.

At the mall, I slid the Cutlass into a slot near the entrance, locked the doors and entered the mall. A few minutes later I had left the film to be developed and was wandering through the mall, killing time.

At this point, I was willing to try anything.

An hour later I picked up the prints and headed for downtown Los Angeles. A close friend of mine, a woman whose sons had played on the same little league team with my son, is an executive at Pacific Bell. We had dated for about two months shortly after my divorce.

I found a parking place in the employee lot and told a pretty receptionist whom I wanted to see. Minutes later I was sitting in the plush office of Lorna Thornberry, admiring her long legs and wondering what life would have been had things worked out between the two of us.

"What brings you to PacBell, Kip?" she asked.

"I need a favor," I said. "I would like to see the records of a girl named Donna Wilson, who was murdered last week at her home in Seal Beach."

"I read about that," she said. "Are you investigating her murder?"

"I'm actually investigating another murder case, but her murder, I feel certain, is tied to the case I'm working."

I gave Lorna Donna's phone number and she picked up her phone and gave instructions to a subordinate. We chatted amiably for a few minutes until the buzzer on her phone interrupted.

She pushed a button and spoke into the intercom, "Bring it in please."

The pretty receptionist brought in a green-lined computer report. She handed it to Lorna who handed it to me without looking at it.

I opened the report and glanced at the numbers and corresponding names.

Donna had called the Surf Sound office shortly after I had called her the day she died. The next entry was the one I was looking for. It was Thad Yates' phone number.

I thanked Lorna for the information, and rose to leave.

"Call me sometime," she said and kissed me on the cheek. "I'm glad we are still friends, and I think of you often. I hope everything goes well for you."

"Couldn't be better," I lied.

I left the Pacific Bell telephone office and headed south towards Toby Smith's home. I guessed that he would be home, knowing his schedule. My mind was racing ahead, trying to think of what I was going to say.

"Toby, Ol' Buddy," I could hear myself saying, "it looks like it's another fine mess you've got me into."

As I drove I thought about the years that we had been friends. He had helped me get through my divorce by inviting me for dinner on many different occasions. We had sat at his dining room table and talked things over.

His wife, Jan, was always encouraging me to go out and have a fling. Like most women, she was sure that I would find another woman that would make up the empty spot left in my heart.

We had gone to basketball games, watched the Dodgers on TV and at Chavez Ravine. We were inseparable for a long time. Toby and Jan didn't have any children. They had decided that children of police officers didn't lead normal lives.

At noon I pulled into the cul-de-sac where Toby lived. His house was the middle one on the left, and I saw his car parked at the curb. It was the Cadillac. I knew now that it was the same car I had seen easing around the corner while I watched from the guard shack at TARA.

Suddenly I noticed Toby's door open and he came out. His copper colored hair glistened in the noon day sun. He waved at Jan, got in the car and started to back out of the driveway. I shaded my face with my left hand and drove on past his house, pulling to the right of the street. I was sure he didn't know it was me, and there was no reason he would recognize the Oldsmobile I was driving.

He turned the corner of the street and was back on a through street as I turned in the cul-de-sac. I sped up and made the same right turn. I watched the Cadillac gain speed as he headed towards Huntington Beach Boulevard. I was careful not to get too close, but stayed on his tail.

He got on the San Diego freeway and headed north. I shadowed him, careful to stay a few car lengths behind. When he got to the 605 he exited to the northbound lanes and I followed.

It didn't occur to me right away that he was leading me towards the place I would have probably gone anyway. Sheriff Thad Yates home in Alhambra.

When he got off the 605 freeway, sometimes called the San Gabriel River Freeway, I knew where he was going. It still didn't seem possible that Toby was mixed up in all of this. I was sad that a good friend had turned on me. Not only turned on me, but apparently tried his damnedest to blow me away.

He parked in the spot where my Chevy had set a few days earlier and walked to the front of Thad Yates house. He rang the doorbell and waited.

I eased to the curb a block away and sat with engine running, watching. Thad Yates opened his own door and the two of them disappeared inside. I killed the engine and took a tape recorder from my briefcase and tucked it under my shirt, flipping the record switch to voice activated.

I started to leave the car, thought better of it and dropped my pants. I taped a smaller, less powerful tape recorder to the back of my thigh on my right leg. I pulled up my pants, picked up my camera bag from the back seat and headed for Yates' house.

The oleanders were in full bloom and I took a deep breath of clean sweet air. I didn't walk up the stone walkway to the front door. Instead, I circled the philodendrons and edged my way around the house, looking for a window where I might eavesdrop.

I bent over low, ran a few yards and dropped to hands and knees beneath a window that I knew was the same room I had stood in a week ago, questioning Thad Yates.

I eased my head up over the stucco and peered in. I could see Yates and Toby talking. Toby appeared to be in charge of the conversation. The window was closed and I could not hear what was being said, but by the expression on Yates' face, I could tell that he was annoyed.

Toby's back was to me and I could not read his lips. I stared hard at Yates' face, trying to read his lips. It was difficult to catch any words, but occasionally I thought Yates mouthed the "f" word.

The conversation between the two ended abruptly and Toby turned his back on Yates and disappeared toward the front of the house. I heard the front door open and could hear Toby's heels clicking on the front entry tile. I heard the Sheriff say something that sounded like "don't come back until you have it," then the sound of Toby's car starting and a small screech of tires as the car rolled away.

Just as I started to turn I felt something poke me hard in the ribs.

"Don't try anything stupid, Stupid," a voice said.

CHAPTER 31

The man holding a gun against my ribs was tall, maybe six inches taller than me. He was thin as a rail and his mustache and goatee made him look even thinner. His dark hair was combed straight back and an evil grin on his face told me that regardless of my martial arts training, I had no chance of taking the gun out of my ribs without getting myself killed.

"Inside, Yardley," he said.

"Oh, you know my name?" I asked.

"I know you, Mister," he said.

We walked around the edge of the philodendrons, retracing my earlier steps around the house. He opened the huge front door with one hand while pointing the gun at my belly button with the other.

"Inside," he said, again.

I went in. Thad Yates stood fifteen feet away from me, a surprised look on his face.

"Yardley," he said. "What brings you back to my humble abode?"

"This goon holding a gun on me," I said, motioning behind me with my thumb.

"Easy, does it, Yardley," the goon said, "I don't have any qualms about shooting private detectives."

"Back off, Bones," Yates said.

"I repeat, Yardley, what brings you to my humble abode?"

"The same thing that brought me here the last time, Yates," I said. "You lied to me about not knowing Donna Wilson. I have proof that you talked to her on the phone the same day she was gunned down."

"Nonsense," he smiled. "I don't know what you're talking about."

"Telephone records," I said. His smile faded.

"Donna Wilson called you not more than two hours before she was killed, according to Pacific Telephone records," I said.

"Even assuming that information is true, Yardley, what does that have to do with your being here? I understand the authorities in Seal Beach want to question you about a man who was killed there last night."

"Sit on it," I said. "You got caught with your pants down, Yates, and your playmate got himself wasted because of it."

"Explain that," he said, smiling again.

"The way I see it, you have been reporting the same marijuana bust over and over, making the newspapers three or four times a month. County Sheriff intercepts another marijuana shipment," I said.

"Why would I do that?" he asked, continuing to smile the same phony politician's smile.

"I guess the publicity is good for your campaign to become the next Governor of this state, Sheriff. The only problem is someone was going to steal your cache."

"Steve Lang had ideas to steal the marijuana you were moving around from place to place, faking new drug busts. He bragged to friends that he was going to make a fortune selling a large amount of pot."

"Lang got crossed up, though, when he went to the wrong guys to sell the dope. He didn't know that a big hairy ape was on your payroll. My guess is that Hair somehow leaked your name and then had to get rid of Lang."

"Lang's girl friend, Donna, put two and two together when she saw Lang's initials on the same bales of pot that you reported "finding". She felt you owed her something since her boyfriend had been killed. She tried to blackmail you and you sent this ugly cadaver here out to shut her up. Am I right, Sheriff?"

"Do you really believe that I am going to confess to murder so that you can capture every word on that tape recorder you have under your shirt?" he said, smiling.

"Take that damned thing, Bones," he motioned to the man who held the gun on me.

"Give it up, Yardley," Bones said.

I unbuttoned my shirt and extracted the small tape recorder.

"Put it down and slide it to me with your foot," Yates said. I did as I was told.

Yates picked it up, flipped the switch to rewind and the small instrument squealed until it clicked. He pushed the play button and Bones voice was clear and distinct, as he said, "Don't try anything stupid, Stupid."

We stood there listening to the instant replay of the past few minutes; Yates with the sickening smile still spread across his chops.

He switched it off and set the recorder on a table.

"Go on with your hypothesis, Yardley," he said. "I don't like to be interviewed on the record."

"The interview is over, Yates," I said. "I don't have time to play games with you. You either have to put a bullet in me, or I'm walking out of here."

I was bluffing, and Yates knew it.

"It's your funeral, Yardley," he said. "If you think I won't let Bones blast you in my living room, you are dumber than you look."

I heard a distinct click from behind me, and knew that Bones would not hesitate.

Discretion is always the better part of valor, I have always heard. I do not relish the thought of dying. My mind raced through a series of events in which I had narrowly escaped death: a fall from a cliff in Yokosuka, Japan, while climbing; a fall on the ship while in the Navy from the top deck to the sixth deck; a dumb stunt when I talked a drunk man into giving me a loaded gun in order to protect his stepson; the many times I had came close to death on the Highway Patrol; and the events of the past few weeks.

"Continue, Yardley," Yates said. "Your theory amuses me."

"I don't know how Hoss's death figures in this," I said. "One thing that I'm sure of, it has something to do with the fact the marijuana was stashed at Tara.

Then there's the beach kid that was killed with my gun. Did you order that one too?"

"Hoss was in my way," Yates said. I felt my heart starting to palpitate. He was actually starting to talk and I might get a confession out of him. The backup tape recorder taped to my calf was silently witnessing what I hoped to be a confession.

"In your way?" I asked. "The way I had it figured, you were partners on this marijuana deal. What do you mean he was in your way?"

"Hoss was in over his head with some dope smugglers," Yates began. "He owed a lot of money and he didn't want to keep the stash for me to use in my publicity gimmick. He felt I should use phony bales. He needed to sell the real stuff to pay off his debts."

"Oh, I see," I broke in. "You needed to keep the real thing because if anyone ever checked the bales your scam would be busted!"

"Now your getting smarter," Yates said. "I kept Hoss out of jail for years, I protected his interest in the nude joints, and he didn't want to play my game."

"So it wasn't the drug lords who bumped Hoss, it was you."

"Not me personally, Yardley," he said. "You know I wouldn't do something like that. I just had some people do it for me. Called in a favor, you might say."

"Toby Smith?" I asked.

"Smith?" he repeated. "He wasn't in on the Hoss hit."

I felt a sigh of relief surge through me. I guess I had pegged the license plate thing wrong. Toby wasn't part of the deal. I was in a hell of a mess here, but I was jumping with joy that Toby wasn't part of the gang of crooks.

"So you had Hair bump Hoss?"

"It didn't take much persuading. Hair married Hoss's ex-wife. He stood to take over control of the nude bars, since Hoss had never changed his will, and everything he had went to his ex-wife," Yates said.

"What about the kid from the beach?" I asked.

"After you started snooping around, Gary thought he could muscle in where Steve Lang left off. He went to Tara and tried to talk Hair into turning on me. Fortunately for me, he got there right before you did. Ernesto killed Gary with your gun and dumped his body in the hole under the barn. And after you escaped from there, we decided to let the police get you out of our hair by giving them the corpse. Hair called the State Police and they found the body."

"And it was this ugly cadaver and Twinkle-Toes who tried to blow me away," I said, careful to keep an eye on the skinny jerk who held the gun on me. I actually hoped he would try to hit me: it would give me a chance to try to get his gun away from him.

He wouldn't fall for it.

"You got out of the hole at Tara," he said, "but I'll lay odds you can't get out of here alive."

"I want you to know that I mailed copies of the negatives to myself, and if anything happens to me, friends of mine will get the negatives," I said, smirking.

"You are dumber than you look, Yardley," Yates said. "I've got a man watching your place now, to put you under arrest for killing Chico."

"By the way, who did blast Chico?" I asked.

"Now wouldn't you like to know?"

I remembered the patrol car that I had seen cruising away from the area. I started having doubts again about Toby. Did he shoot Chico?

"O.K. Yates," I said, sighing. "What are your plans for me? Do you think you can hang Chico's death on me? It wasn't my gun that got him."

"You are going to have an accident," he said, smiling that sickening sweet politician's smile. "You came here making false accusations, creating a ruckus. We tried to detain you and you got tough with us. We put you in the wine cellar to hold you until city police could arrive, and you accidentally knocked a gas pipe loose trying to get out. The gas overcame you."

He opened the tape recorder, removed the tape, stuffed it in his shirt pocket and tossed the recorder back to me. I caught it and stuck it in my camera bag.

"I gave you credit for being smarter than you are, Yardley," he said. "You could have joined me instead of fighting me. The trouble with guys like you is you never know which side of your bread is buttered."

"Put him in the wine cellar, Bones," he said. "Kick that gas pipe loose and in a few hours we'll shut off the main and go in after him. He should be nice and pickled by then. That should coincide with Toby Smith's return."

I wondered what he meant by that, but didn't have time to elaborate or question him. Bones was escorting me to the building I had seen on my first trip, staying just far enough behind me to avoid any of my intentions. My intention was to stay alive as long as possible, so I followed his instructions.

The building had been built as a garage with an apartment over it, but the ground floor had been excavated to form a wine cellar, and then cemented back. The wine cellar was a ten by ten hole in the ground, cement walls lined with wine racks. On one wall was a door that opened to street level on the west side, through a narrow five-foot walk in passageway.

Against one wall, up against the wine racks, was an ancient, chest type freezer. I could hear its motor humming along in the quietness of the cellar. Someone had removed the twist out legs and replaced them with casters, apparently in an effort to make the heavy freezer easier to move.

The capped stub of a gas line ran through one wall. Apparently it had been used at some time or another for a gas operated coolant system to keep the wine cellar at the desired temperature.

There were no lights in the wine cellar. The door was steel and six inches thick. The only light in the room came from a darkened glass, six inches square, and the thickness of the door. Someone had been serious about their wine. A few dusty bottles of wine still adorned the wine racks, their leaded corks glistening wetly in the dampness of the cellar.

Bones held the gun on me with one hand and kneeling, used a pipe wrench to remove the cap slowly from the gas line. I could hear gas hissing through the threads before he had the cap completely off.

"Let's see you escape this time, Houdini," Bones said, laughing.

He finished removing the cap, stuffed it in his pocket and backed out the door.

CHAPTER 32

My thoughts were immediately racing around in my head as my eyes searched the room for something to seal the gas pipe. What I needed was a stopper of some kind, like a cork.

Bingo! The corks in the wine bottles! I was amazed at how stupid I had been, almost at a panic stage, trying to figure a way to stop the gas from coming in. I was also astounded at how stupid Yates and Bones had been.

I grabbed a bottle of Lafitte Rothschild 1909 from a rack and quickly peeled the lead seal of the cork. Then I realized I didn't have anything with which to remove the cork from the bottle.

Hating myself for the waste of such an expensive wine, I broke the neck of the bottle off on the edge of the freezer, cutting my finger in the process, and using the heel of my shoe, broke the glass from around the cork. I could smell the sickening smell of natural gas, getting stronger every minute.

I tried the cork in the pipe. It was an eighth of an inch too small all around. I picked up a piece of the lead foil and wrapped it around the cork, then jammed lead and cork into the pipe. It fit better, but was still leaking, I could hear the hiss of the deadly gas escaping around my makeshift seal. Maybe Yates and Bones weren't so stupid after all. Maybe it was me.

My breathing was becoming more and more difficult. No more than three minutes had passed since the door slammed shut, but the escaping gas was making me nauseous and my breath was getting heavier.

I knew that the makeshift seal wasn't going to do the trick, and I had run out of resources. I glanced around the room again, looking for something to help seal the pipe. My eyes fell on my camera bag. I had empty plastic film cartridges in the bag, but I knew without checking that they were too big around to stuff in the pipe.

Suddenly an idea started to surface, like the creature from the black lagoon, in my muddled mind. I would simply blast my way out!

Quickly I unplugged the freezer and used my pocketknife to cut through the insulation, twisting and bending the wire until it was loose. I took a long shutter cable from my camera bag and twisted one side of the 110 volt wire around the end, tested the distance the plunger moved, and placed the other wire an eighth of an inch from the first.

By pressing the plunger on the shutter cable, I could make the two wires touch. I opened the lid on the dilapidated freezer and looked inside. There were some forgotten freezer bags of meat and some frozen vegetables that I quickly removed and tossed aside.

I plugged the freezer cord back into the wall outlet and carefully got in the freezer, gently playing out the shutter cable as I did. The interior of the freezer was big enough for me to sit down, draw up my knees and close the lid. I made sure there were no latches that would prevent me from getting out of the freezer once the lid was closed, then gently lowered the lid until the rubber seal completely blacked out what little light there was.

I was conscious of the fact that if this didn't work, or if the seals on the freezer chest were not tight enough, I would either die a terrible death from the gas, or breath in a lung full of fiery flames.

I'm not a very religious person, but in that split second before I pushed the plunger on the shutter cable, I wondered whether I would go to heaven or to hell.

CHAPTER 33

The roar inside the freezer echoed back and forth in my head. I didn't feel any flash of heat, but I could smell burning rubber. The stench of burning paint mixed with the vinegary sweet smell of wine permeated my senses.

I didn't realize the freezer was moving for a few seconds after the blast. Suddenly, however, I felt a hard bump on my backside and the definite sense of movement. I cautiously drew my legs up under me, put my hands on the underneath side of the freezer lid and lifted, slowly at first, then shoved the lid fully open.

Bright sunlight poured into my eyes. I raised my head and looked over the edge of the freezer to see the blazing wine cellar disappearing rapidly away from me.

Startled, I pulled myself up on the sides of the freezer and looked around.

The force of the explosion had opened the door and hurtled the ancient, blazing freezer out the open door, and the freezer with me in it was rapidly rolling down a steep hill away from Thad Yates's house. I turned to look in the direction the freezer was rolling, just in time to see a car approaching from a side street at a rapid rate.

"EEEEEYAAAHHHHHH!" I screamed.

"EEEEEYAAAHHHHHH!" I heard the driver of the red convertible scream.

The freezer, with me in it, narrowly missed the car as it sped through the intersection.

I and my downhill racing freezer picked up speed. I could hear the clackety, clackety of the worn rubber caster wheels as we sped down the hill.

Directly ahead, the street ended, forming a tee with an intersecting street. I thought about jumping out slightly before the freezer crossed the intersecting street, roared up a driveway, ripped through a grape-stake fence, and headed for the backyard.

Hanging onto the edges of the freezer, knuckles white with the grip, I sat frozen as the freezer soared off into the deep end of a large swimming pool.

I caught a glimpse of a fat woman wearing a bikini that covered very little of her big body. She had blue hair and wore sunglasses. Her mouth opened in a hysterical screech, but I didn't hear it.

The water splashed high over my head, drenching me. I could hear the hiss as the cold water put out the burning paint.

I kicked my way out of the freezer as it sank slowly to the bottom of the pool.

The fat lady was pointing at me with one hand, her other hand over her mouth, making gurgling sounds. I swam towards her and she retreated, looking at me like I was the Loch Ness monster, rising from the drain of her swimming pool.

"Can I use your phone?" I gasped

"ARRRGGHG," she said, still pointing at me.

CHAPTER 34

I sat in my soaking wet clothes, drinking a beer, trying not to make eye contact with the fat lady who had calmed down enough to let me use her phone. She was smiling at me, a huge, large mouthed, pearly-toothed smile, and offering me something to eat.

I was thankful when a detective-sergeant from the LAPD showed up, rang the bell, and was ushered in by the fat lady.

I had untaped the small recorder from behind my thigh and using a hair dryer borrowed from my new-found friend, had dried it out pretty thoroughly. I replaced the small tape spool and to my amazement, it played.

After taking a few preliminary notes, the LA cop, Jeff Burnside, got on the phone and called the district attorney. I knew I would have to go downtown and answer a lot of questions, but I also knew that Yates would be arrested and held for arraignment.

Burnside left and I thanked the fat lady for all of her kindness, and started to leave. Thank God this case was about over.

"You're not leaving so soon are you?" the fat lady asked.

"Well, I think the police want me to go downtown and fill out some paper work," I said, wanting very badly to just go home and soak in my tub for about three weeks.

"But I was going to play the piano for you," she moaned.

"I would really like to hear you play," I lied. "But really, I...."

She didn't let me finish. She scooted away like a large crab on a hot rock and sat down at the piano.

I thought of an old saying I had learned while watching a Dodger ball game. Vin Scully was announcing the game and I was listening to it on a small portable radio.

The Dodgers were down 4 to 3 in the bottom of the ninth with two out and no one on base.

Scully said, "It ain't over till the fat lady sings."

Just then she started singing.

"There's a blue moon over my shoulder, and a new love here in my heart."

I left.

CHAPTER 35

It was nearly six when I left the downtown L.A. precinct office. Yates was in jail being held for payment of a million-dollar bond.

Hair was last seen riding a chopper up Pacific Coast Highway. The Highway Patrol was hot on his tail.

I had something I needed to do, an answer that I had to have. I headed for Toby Smith's house.

He answered the door the second time I pushed the doorbell button, and stood there, like Howdy Doody, looking at me.

"Well if it isn't my old pal Kip Yardley," he smiled.

"Can we talk?"

"Sure, come on in buddy," he said, in that high pitched nasal twang that I had known for so long.

"One question."

"Shoot."

"Were you in on the Hoss hit?" I couldn't put it any more bluntly.

"What?"

"You heard me," I said. "Did you have anything to do with Hoss's death or the death of Donna Wilson or Steve Lang?"

"Whoa," he said. "Have you been smoking that whacky tobacky we found in your freezer?"

My mind raced back to the night I had been beaned and someone had ransacked my apartment but left the marijuana rolled up in a newspaper in my freezer.

"So it was you!"

"So it was me what?"

"You beaned me and searched my apartment looking for the pictures!" I screeched.

"I didn't bean anybody," he said. "We found the marijuana the night you got beaned. Your next-door neighbor called us right after he called the ambulance that took you to the hospital. I rewired your phone and made a call to headquarters."

"I figured the pot had something to do with the case you were working, so I put it back where it was. I didn't realize you were going to smoke it!"

"I haven't smoked anything," I protested.

"Well what the hell are you accusing me of beaning you for? You know I wouldn't kill anybody, much less Hoss MacMillan. He was a friend of mine."

"But the license plates," I muttered.

"What the hell license plates are you talking about," he asked.

I told him about the association I had made between the word raingear and the license plate number of his car, which was the combination of the raingear locker at the old patrol station.

"Hell, I could have saved you a lot of trouble if you had asked me," he started. "I followed you to TARA the day you got thrown in the cellar. You're questions about Hoss McMillan's death told me you were going out there. After you left, I thought the police barricades would still be up, so I drove out there to see if I could get them to let you in."

"You must have got there right after I did!" I said.

"I saw your car, and I pulled over thinking you might still be in it," he grinned. "When I didn't see you, I left."

"And when I told you about the license plate you didn't make the connection because you didn't realize it was your car pulling away?" I asked, incredulously.

"Honest," he laughed, "I didn't even think about it being my car you were trying to identify."

I felt so stupid I could have cried. I didn't want him to see the look in my eyes, so I turned away. Then I thought about seeing him at Yates' house right before I got caught looking in the window.

"But you were at Yates' place right before I got caught looking in the window. I saw you talking to him!"

"I went there and accused him of some of the things you proved," Toby said. "He kicked me out and told me not to come back without proof!"

"Well, I'm glad it wasn't you!" I said, with a lump in my throat.

"Forget it, Ol' Buddy," he said. "Come on in and have a beer with me. We'll watch the ballgame."

"Some other time, pal," I said. I had other plans for this night.

My plans were to call on a long legged woman who wanted me to swim in her pool with no clothes on.

THE END

ABOUT THE AUTHOR

Don Yarber was born in Harrisburg, IL and attended college at El Camino College in Torrance, CA where he studied Journalism. "Bodies and Beaches" is his first attempt at writing a classic PI novel.

WHAT PEOPLE ARE SAYING ABOUT BODIES AND BEACHES

Scott Meredith Literary Agency:

"Stands well above most first novel attempts"

Richard S. Prather (author of Shell Scott mysteries):

Bottom line: Bodies and Beaches is a good job, with a likable lead and a lot of interesting action I enjoyed reading, and you write very well indeed. Verdict: Well done!